To See With the Heart

To See With the Heart

The Life of Sitting Bull

▰▰▰

Judith St. George

G. P. Putnam's Sons   New York

G. P. Putnam's Sons, a division of The Putnam & Grosset Group,
200 Madison Avenue, New York, NY 10016.
G. P. Putnam's Sons, Reg. U.S. Pat. & Tm. Off.
Published simultaneously in Canada
Printed in the United States of America
Book design by Patrick Collins
The text is set in Aster.

Library of Congress Cataloging-in-Publication Data
St. George, Judith, 1931–   To see with the heart :
the life of Sitting Bull / Judith St. George.   p.   cm.
Includes bibliographical references and index.
1. Sitting Bull, 1834?–1890—Juvenile literature.   2. Dakota
Indians—Juvenile literature.   3. Hunkpapa Indians—Biography—
Juvenile literature.   4. Hunkpapa Indians—History—Juvenile
literature.   5. Sitting Bull, 1834?–1890.   I. Title.
E99.D1S6183   978'.004975'0092—dc20   [B]   95-458 CIP AC
ISBN 0-399-22930-2

10   9   8   7   6   5   4   3   2   1

First impression

To Hannah Katherine, with love

Introduction

While researching and writing a biography of Crazy Horse several years ago, I was drawn again and again to the compelling figure of Sitting Bull. Because he was photographed only during his last years, I had always pictured him as elderly and grim-faced. But the Sitting Bull I came to know, if only slightly, was a vital and vigorous warrior and leader who cared deeply for his family and his people. The more I learned about him, the more appealing the prospect of getting to the heart of the man became.

There were two avenues open to discovering the real Sitting Bull. The first was the Walter S. Campbell Collection at the University of Oklahoma. During the 1920s and 1930s, Walter Campbell, whose pen name was Stanley Vestal, extensively interviewed Sitting Bull's contemporaries, particularly his nephews One Bull and White Bull. Although some details, such as Sitting Bull's birth date, varied, their accounts revealed fewer discrepancies than I would have expected.

My second approach to Sitting Bull was to travel in his footsteps. My husband, David, and I drove some two thousand miles through the northern Great Plains, from South Dakota's Grand River up into the North Dakota Badlands, west to Montana's Yellowstone River country, and from there, north into Canada. We tramped around battle sites and camping grounds; we visited trading posts and forts; we crossed and recrossed the Missouri River. The vastness of the country, the rolling treeless plains, the wide-open skies, the sudden storms, all made Sitting Bull come alive in a way that books never could.

My thanks go first to David, who helped me decipher and collate hundreds of pages of hand-written notes in the Campbell Collection and who was driver and photographer extraordinaire on our Great Plains adventure. My thanks also go to those men and women we met on our journey who so willingly gave of their time and wisdom to answer questions and provide insights and information. They all helped me in my quest to find the real Sitting Bull.

◄ 1 ►

On the warpath
I give place to none
With dauntless courage I live.

Hunkpapa War Song

Sitting Bull's Hunkpapa tribe of Sioux was camped on the Powder River in the year 1845. Only fourteen years old, Sitting Bull was known to the people of his village as Slow. It wasn't that he was slow moving. Far from it. Rather, the name came from the way that he took his time making up his mind. And once he made up his mind, there was no changing it.

For two days, Slow's father and twenty other warriors had been making preparations to stage a raid on their enemy, the Crows. After packing their war clothes, shields, lances, bows and arrows, war paint, warbonnets, whistles, food, and food bowls, the men rode out of camp leading their trained war-horses behind them.

Slow watched them go. He longed to be a warrior. For years he had admired the brave warriors of the village as they re-

1

turned from battle to be greeted by songs and cheers. Going on the warpath, stealing horses, counting coup, and bringing back enemy scalps—that was where the glory lay.

Slow made up his mind to ride after them. He didn't stop to think that he was the only son in the family or that his parents and his two sisters might worry. The time had come to prove himself as a warrior and that was all he cared about. As soon as the men were out of sight, Slow packed his belongings, mounted the sturdy gray pony that his father had given him, and followed the war party's trail.

Probably none of the warriors was surprised when Slow caught up to them. "No boy was a full-fledged man until he had been out with a war-party," a fellow tribesman said, and Slow was no exception. And there was no point in trying to talk him into going back. Everyone, especially his father, knew that Slow was too strong-willed to give up now that he had come this far. At least the older men would make sure that he was out of danger by having him watch the horses or carry water.

It wasn't long before a scout rode back to report that he had sighted a Crow war party. Quickly the Hunkpapas dressed, painted for war, tied their hair in knots over their foreheads, and hid behind a hillock. Peering out, they saw the unsuspecting Crows approach. Mounted on his gray pony that he had painted red, Slow also saw them coming. This was it, the chance to prove himself. He broke out into the open.

Hopo! Charge! Down the hill he plunged, shrieking and war whooping. As he galloped toward the enemy, the rest of the Hunkpapas burst out of hiding and charged too. Immediately, the Crows spread into a defensive line, all but one Crow who fled.

2

Slow saw him. This Crow would be his. With his body painted yellow and dressed in only a breechcloth, moccasins, and strings of beads, Slow gave chase. He pushed his pony hard until he caught up to the Crow. Swinging his tomahawk, he knocked the Crow off his mount.

"*On-hey!* I, Slow, have conquered this enemy," he shouted.

Although the other Hunkpapas finished off the Crow, as the first to strike the enemy, Slow had counted first coup. Later he said, "When fourteen years of age I went on my first warpath against a neighboring tribe. I distinguished myself for my bravery." He wasn't boasting. He was simply recounting what he had accomplished, as all warriors were expected to do. Many years later, a kinsman called Slow's coup his "first brave deed."

What a victorious raid it turned out to be. The Hunkpapas killed all the Crows except for four, who escaped. Although the villagers turned out to praise and cheer the returning warriors, it was Slow who was hailed as the hero, as well he should have been. He was only fourteen and had already counted his first coup.

That night Slow's father, Sitting Bull, threw a feast for all the people in honor of his son's new standing as a warrior. He painted Slow's face and body black as a sign of victory and placed a white eagle feather upright in his hair to celebrate his first coup. After giving Slow's gray pony, as well as other fine horses, to the needy ones, Sitting Bull led Slow around the camp circle on a handsome new bay. Slow sat proud and tall as his family and friends acclaimed his courage and sang his praises.

Sitting Bull also presented his son with a lance and a shield.

The ashwood lance, which Slow's mother had decorated with blue and white beads, was more than seven feet long. A notched iron blade was fastened to its tip, and a golden eagle feather to its base.

The shield, which his father had designed according to a vision, gave Slow special sacred powers. Made of tough buffalo hide with a birdlike figure painted in the center, the shield was red to symbolize the sun, blue for the sky, green for the earth, and yellow for the rock. The four eagle feathers that hung from the frame promised success in the four directions, east, south, west, and north. It was Slow's most treasured possession, and he carried it into battle for the rest of his fighting days.

But Slow received a more valuable gift from his father than a new horse, a lance, or a shield. It was a gift that he would bear with pride for the rest of his life.

"My son has struck the enemy," Sitting Bull announced to the gathering. "He is brave. I call him Tatanka-Iyotanka."

Slow said nothing. His heart was too full. His father had given him his own name, Sitting Buffalo Bull. At the same time, his father took a new name for himself, Jumping Bull.

Sitting Bull was a fitting name for the young warrior who already had shown himself to be as unyielding and courageous as a buffalo bull. A stubborn animal of great strength and endurance, a buffalo bull would set a course and never turn back or give up, no matter what the danger. In a blizzard the buffalo would face squarely into the wind and wait out the storm.

"Sitting Bull did not imitate *any* man," a Hunkpapa warrior declared. "He imitated the buffalo. There was nothing secondhand about Sitting Bull."

4

◄ 2 ►

"Alone in the wilderness I roam
With much hardships in the wilderness I roam."
A wolf said this to me.

Sitting Bull's Song
Dedicated to the Wolf Tribe

Sitting Bull soon lived up to the promise of his new name. The following year, 1846, he and his family were camped with their Hunkpapa band on the Musselshell River when scouts warned that a war party of an unknown tribe was spying on them. This time Sitting Bull didn't have to sneak out of camp to join the war party. He was fifteen now, and a respected warrior.

Carrying his new lance and shield, Sitting Bull, with fourteen other Hunkpapas, rode up to the surrounding hills to see who these strangers were and what they wanted. Suddenly, some twenty Flatheads galloped out of hiding in a surprise attack. It was an ambush! As the Hunkpapas scrambled to counter the charge, the Flatheads dismounted, lined up behind their horses, and began firing.

5

Sitting Bull never considered his first coup to be triumph enough. He craved higher war honors than that. Calling out to his fellow warriors to stay back, he rode out alone. Heading his warhorse toward the enemy, he trotted along the length of their line, within firing distance. As he dashed the daring line, his Hunkpapa comrades shouted his name over and over to empower him: "Sitting Bull! Sitting Bull!"

And he was empowered. Without flinching, he heard the bullets whistle all around him, but he wasn't hit. Suddenly he felt a burning stab. A bullet had grazed his right foot. The wound wasn't serious, and he hardly noticed the pain in the excitement of the fight that followed. The other Hunkpapas joined him, and the battle was fierce. Finally, with both sides having lost about half of their warriors, mostly to wounds, the Flatheads withdrew and the Hunkpapas rode back to camp.

Once again, Sitting Bull was the hero of the day. Once again, the story of his bravery was told and retold. Once again, he was presented with a feather to wear in his hair. The tip of this feather, however, was red, to let the world know that he had been wounded in battle. There began to be talk in the village. This courageous young man would go far. He was only fifteen, and already his bravery and daring had elevated him above the others.

It seemed that the animal world would have agreed, making a prophecy of its own. Sitting Bull told how soon after he was awarded his red-tipped feather, he was hunting in the thickest part of a cottonwood forest when he heard a voice crying out in pain. Someone needed help. Following the voice, he was surprised to come upon a wolf wounded by two arrows.

"Boy, if you will relieve me your name shall be great," the wolf promised.

Sympathizing with the animal in its agony, Sitting Bull never hesitated. Just a short while ago, he, too, had been wounded. He pulled out the arrows, tended to the wounds, and sent the wolf on its way.

When he was alone, Sitting Bull thought about what the wolf had told him. In his heart, he may have suspected that greatness lay ahead. Now, from the wolf's promise, he knew for certain that fame and leadership of his people were his destiny. To express his pleasure, he composed a song about the solitary life of a wolf and dedicated it to the wolf tribe.

> *"Alone in the wilderness I roam*
> *With much hardships in the wilderness I roam."*
> *A wolf said this to me.*

◂ 3 ▸

Friends, whoever runs away,
He is a woman, they say;
Therefore, through many trials,
My life is short!

Strong Heart Song

By the time Sitting Bull had gone from his teen years into his twenties, he was five feet, ten inches tall, brawny and muscular, with a thick chest and a large head. His penetrating dark eyes, prominent cheekbones, broad strong nose, and firm mouth made him look stubbornly determined, which he was. He parted his shoulder-length hair in the middle, often braiding one side and leaving the other side loose, with the center part painted red. His voice was deep and firm.

In 1851 Sitting Bull married his true love, a young woman from his village. "When I attained the age of twenty years," he said, "I ended my single blessedness by my successful winning of the hand of Tatiyopa."

Sitting Bull was successful in battle, too, and took pride in always riding out in front of the others. A fellow warrior de-

8

scribed Sitting Bull's role as a "fronter": "Every time Sitting Bull got there first and so wherever he was and whatever he did his name was great everywhere. Whenever Sitting Bull [was] at war he never try to hold in his horse—but wants to get there first."

Sitting Bull's bravery and daring as a warrior soon became well known. His comrades could strike fear in their enemies' hearts by attacking with the cry, "We are Sitting Bull's boys!"

Before long Sitting Bull was asked to join two secret *akicita* societies, the Kit Foxes and the Strong Hearts. Members of *akicita* societies guarded the people, enforced order in the camp, and prevented eager young warriors from breaking ranks and ruining an ambush or a buffalo surround. Sitting Bull, Gall, Crow King, and other warrior-friends went on to found the Midnight Strong Heart Society, which met secretly at midnight for feasts, ceremonies, fellowship, singing, and recounting of brave deeds.

Like the other Strong Heart members, Sitting Bull's battle dress was a long red sash and a crow-feathered cap with two buffalo horns and a trailing eagle-feather tail. In combat he often wore the red sash over his shoulder, staking both ends into the ground. Forced to stand in one place, he was committed to fighting until a fellow warrior withdrew the stakes . . . or he was killed.

In 1856, soon after becoming a sash-wearer, Sitting Bull joined a large war party. Setting out from their camp just north of the Yellowstone River, called Elk River by the Sioux, the warriors headed west to steal Crow horses. Shortly after they reached Crow country, they spotted a band of Crows guarding a herd of horses. Several Hunkpapa warriors crept into the Crow camp that night and made off with the horses. As they drove the slow-moving herd toward home, the rest of the war party stayed behind, anticipating that before long the Crows would come after their missing horses. And they did. The sun had barely risen when the Crows, in full war regalia, charged over the brow of the hill.

Sitting Bull, who wore his Strong Heart warbonnet and red sash, was waiting for them, along with the other Hunkpapa warriors. While most of the Crows pulled their horses up short at the sight of the armed and combat-ready Hunkpapas, three of their leaders raced on ahead. As one Crow leader dashed into the Hunkpapa line and counted two coups, Loud Bear grabbed the long tail of the leader's warbonnet and ripped it off. It was such an out-of-the-ordinary stunt that the year 1856 was known in the Hunkpapa picture calendar as "The-Winter-When-the-War-Bonnet-Was-Torn."

The second Crow leader killed the Hunkpapa warrior Paints Brown. One death and two coups counted against them was too much for Sitting Bull. The Crows were, after all, nothing but cowardly women. Carrying his sacred shield and a newly acquired smoothbore muzzle-loading rifle, Sitting Bull jumped off his horse.

"Come on!" he called out to the third Crow leader. "I'll fight you. I am Sitting Bull!"

The Crow, whose red shirt trimmed with ermine marked him as a chief, dismounted, too. Quickly the Hunkpapas and the Crows lined up opposite each other with enough space left in the middle for the two warriors to face off. Sitting Bull ran forward. But the Crow had already raised his flintlock gun. Stopping in his tracks, Sitting Bull crouched and threw up his shield just as the Crow fired. The bullet ripped through Sitting Bull's shield and into his foot, furrowing a deep gash from toe to heel. Although blood streamed from the wound, Sitting Bull never hesitated. He aimed, pulled the trigger, and shot the Crow through the gut, killing him.

Despite the searing pain, Sitting Bull hobbled over to the fallen Crow, plunged in his knife to make certain that he was dead, and then scalped him, thus capturing the Crow chief's spirit. With the chieftain's scalp in his possession, Sitting Bull calmly mounted his horse and rejoined the war party as if nothing were amiss. But his fighting was finished for that day.

When something was excellent, it was called *sha*, red. Sitting Bull's killing of the Crow chief in single combat was *sha-sha*, very red. Sitting Bull's nephew always said that his uncle's daring challenge to fight one-on-one with guns was Sitting Bull's "bravest deed." But he paid a heavy price. Because the bullet wound never healed properly, he was forced to walk on the ball of his foot with a limping gait for the rest of his life. Nevertheless, he early on made up his mind that his injury wouldn't hold him back. And it didn't. He never used a cane, and from time to time he even won footraces.

The following year, 1857, Sitting Bull saw everything come together, just as the wolf had promised. First he became war chief of the Midnight Strong Heart Society, and then his fellow warriors Gall, Black Bird, Brave Thunder, and Strikes-the-Kettle proposed his name to be war chief of all the Hunkpapas.

There was little opposition to his election. How could there be? Sitting Bull was the greatest Hunkpapa warrior in the memory of any of his people. At a tribal gathering held near the confluence of the Grand and Missouri rivers, they voiced their approval. The campsite wasn't far from where Sitting Bull had been born in March 1831, the year the Hunkpapas called "The-Winter-When-Yellow-Eyes-Murdered-an-Indian."

In a special ceremony, Sitting Bull was installed as Hunkpapa war chief. First he smoked a sacred pipe decorated with porcupine quills and duck feathers. He next sucked sweet grass from a cup of water, which committed him always to tell the truth. He was given a cane, not because of his limp, but as a token that he would live to be so old that he would need a cane for walking.

Filled with pride, his wife, his parents, and his two sisters were spectators at the impressive ceremony. What an honor! Here he was, only in his twenties, and he had risen to the highest warrior rank in the Hunkpapa tribe.

Sitting Bull realized that he couldn't rely on his past brave deeds. In order to keep his chieftainship, he would have to lead victorious war parties. A war chief led not by command, but because his men were willing to follow him. Sitting Bull was very much aware that he would have to prove himself over and over again in the years to come. Perhaps it was just as well that he didn't know just how perilous those years would be.

◄ 4 ►

Crows cried!
Crows cried!

Hunkpapa Victory Song
over the Crows

The imes were good for Sitting Bull in the 1850s. As Hunkpapa war chief, he earned greater and greater prestige by leading successful raids against the Crows and the Assiniboines. But he suffered tragedy as well. His beloved young wife died giving birth to their only child, a son. Four years later the young boy fell ill and died, too. Sitting Bull had spent many afternoons with his son, seated on a buffalo robe in the shade, singing, talking, playing, and teaching him to dance.

Heartbroken at the death of his child, Sitting Bull went into mourning. He wailed and cried, didn't eat for four days, let his hair hang loose, wore old rags, covered himself with dust, and went barefoot. To give his life meaning, he adopted his sister Good Feather's son, four-year-old One Bull, who was just the age of the child he had lost. Sitting Bull showered One Bull

13

with all the affection that he would have lavished on his own son.

During that same year, the restless young warriors in Sitting Bull's camp planned a raid against the Hohes, as the Hunkpapas called the Assiniboines. Even though he was still mourning, Sitting Bull smoked the war pipe that was offered to him and joined the war party as a way to ease his grief.

Sighting a Hohe band just below Poplar Creek on the Missouri River, the Hunkpapas attacked in force. They chased the Hohes across a shallow lake, their horses half running and half swimming. Sitting Bull, who wore his Strong Heart sash and bonnet, counted a first coup on a Hohe in the water and another first coup at the water's edge. But in the cross fire that followed, his horse was shot out from under him.

Wading out of the water on foot, Sitting Bull saw that his fellow warriors had surrounded a young Hohe boy. They had already killed the boy's father, mother, and two brothers. Dry-eyed and armed with only a small bow and arrow, the thirteen-year-old boy stood his ground. Death awaited him, and he knew it.

Eight Hunkpapas had been killed in the fighting. The Hohe boy deserved to die. But as Sitting Bull came limping toward him, the boy saw something in the war chief's face that touched him. Sitting Bull may have glanced at him sympathetically. Or his expression might have softened when he witnessed how bravely the youngster faced death. Whatever the bond, the boy turned to Sitting Bull, threw his arms around him, and cried, "Big brother!"

No doubt the death of his own son was sorely on Sitting

Bull's mind. His son might have grown up to be as courageous as this young boy. Sitting Bull moved forward and shielded the Hohe from the angry Hunkpapa warriors.

"Don't shoot," he ordered. "This boy is too brave to die. I have no brother. I take this one for my brother. Let him live."

The warriors were astonished. The boy would have killed them if he could have. He was the enemy and would grow up to fight against them in future battles. They argued against Sitting Bull's foolishness. Arguments were nothing new. Sitting Bull and his comrades were the Icira band of the Hunkpapa Sioux tribe, Icira meaning "always disputing one another."

Their protests were to no avail anyway. Sitting Bull's mind was made up, and that was that. Finally, the hot-tempered warriors agreed to spare the Hohe's life. After finding another horse, Sitting Bull mounted and pulled the boy up behind him for the ride back to camp.

That night in a formal adoption ceremony, Sitting Bull dressed the young Hohe in new clothes, painted his face, gave away horses in his name, and invited the people to a feast. In many ways the celebration was similar to Sitting Bull's first-coup celebration years ago.

Most of the Hunkpapas were sure that the boy would run back to his people as soon as he could. To their surprise, he stayed on to become a lifelong and much loved member of Sitting Bull's family. Some called him Stays-Back because he refused to go home. Others called him Kills-Often because he grew up to be such a fine warrior. To commemorate the adoption, the year 1857 in the Hunkpapa picture calendar was called "The-Winter-When-Kills-Often-Was-Brought-Home."

15

Two years later, in June of 1859, Sitting Bull and his family, including Kills-Often, were headed west with their Icira band to establish a new camp. Although they were crossing the rolling, treeless plains close by two towering bluffs called Rainy Buttes, for a change the day was warm and sunny, and the people were traveling at a lazy pace. Suddenly from behind a knoll fifty war-painted Crows came galloping toward them.

"Yip-yip-yip!" they shrieked.

Before the Hunkpapas could marshal their forces, the Crows killed a young Hunkpapa boy who was leading the line of march on his pony. Outraged, the warriors rallied and counterattacked in what became a running battle. First one Crow was killed, and then another, until all the Crows were in retreat. The Crow chief Bird-Claw-Necklace behaved just the way the Hunkpapas would expect a Crow to behave. He wailed and cried as they cut him down.

Although most of the Crows fled, one warrior's horse gave out and he found himself on his feet, surrounded by hostile Hunkpapas. Sitting Bull's father, Jumping Bull, dismounted and walked toward the Crow. He had been in such pain from a toothache that earlier he had said that he didn't care whether he lived or not.

"Leave him to me!" Jumping Bull called out, although he needn't have. No one ever interfered when two warriors engaged in single combat.

Face-to-face both men went for their knives. But the sheath of Jumping Bull's knife had slipped behind his back, and he couldn't reach it. Not waiting for the old man to retrieve his knife, the Crow stabbed him in the neck and breast. Jumping

Bull slumped to the ground. Leaning over, the Crow thrust his knife so deeply into Jumping Bull's skull that the blade broke off. Then he turned and ran away.

While the Hunkpapa warriors gave furious chase, someone found Sitting Bull and told him what had happened. His blood hot, Sitting Bull quickly overtook the Crow on his swift war-horse Bloated Jaw and knocked him to the ground with his lance. By the time Sitting Bull had leapt from his horse to finish off his father's killer, the Crow was dead from a hail of Hunkpapa arrows and bullets. In a rage, Sitting Bull mutilated and cut up the Crow's body to make sure that when he entered the next world he would be crippled and powerless.

White Bull later told how Sitting Bull's heart was so bad at the cowardly killing of his father that he single-handedly stormed the enemy lines. "Sitting Bull went on and killed five or six more Crows 'till the Hunkpapas brought him back thinking the danger too great."

In revenge for Jumping Bull's death, plans were made that night to kill three Crow women and a Crow boy who had been taken prisoner in the fight. But Sitting Bull's anger had passed. All that was left was an overwhelming sadness at the loss of his father. This was the man who had showed him how to make a bow and arrow, who had given him his first pony, who, by his own example, had taught him what it was to be generous. Above all, this was the man who had loved him so much that he had given him his own name.

But Jumping Bull was gone, and the death of the Crows wouldn't bring him back. Besides, Sitting Bull felt pity for the captives. They, too, had lost loved ones in the battle.

Sitting Bull had learned his lesson in generosity well. "Take good care of the women and boy and let them live," he told those who were prepared to kill the Crows. "It may be you have captured them for my sake but don't harm them. My father is a man and death is his."

Later that summer, Sitting Bull not only arranged to have the four captives taken home, but he saw to it that they were given horses as well. And following in the footsteps of his father, who had bestowed his name on his son, Sitting Bull, in turn, gave his father's honored name to his adopted brother. From that time on, the young Hohe was known to the Hunkpapas as Jumping Bull.

◄ 5 ►

Here am I, behold me
I am the sun, behold me.

Sun Dance Song

Sitting Bull was master of many talents and knew it. "For my part, (not to flatter myself)," he remarked, "in the minds and hearts of my fellow tribesmen, as regards my attainments and accomplishments on the war-path, hunting and acts of kindness and other ways, proved to be more than satisfactory to all concerned."

It was true. Sitting Bull was more than a great warrior in a warrior nation. He was a great hunter in a nation that hunted to survive. "When I was ten years old, I was famous as a hunter," Sitting Bull recalled. "My specialty was buffalo calves." Being generous had always been his other specialty. "I gave what I killed to the poor," he added.

For the hunt Sitting Bull dressed in only a breechcloth and moccasins. With his hair tied behind his ears and his face, arms, and legs painted red, he would urge his buffalo runner into the herd. A fellow hunter described Sitting Bull's remarkable strength: "Sitting Bull shot the arrow clear through the buffalo and the arrow sticks in the ground on the other side."

Sitting Bull may have hunted buffalo with zeal, but he also regarded the buffalo as his brother. When he came upon a buffalo's bleached bones on the plains, he would turn the skull to face the sun. "Friends, we must honor these bones," he would tell his companions. "These are the bones of those who gave their flesh to keep us alive last winter."

Blessed with a powerful singing voice, Sitting Bull was also a gifted composer in a nation that had a song for every occasion: courtship, marriage, birth, death, welcome, farewell, war, peace, victory, defeat. Not every song had words. In some songs, "the words were in the heart," a fellow Hunkpapa explained.

Another Hunkpapa praised Sitting Bull's musical skills: "He was a great singer and could imitate the singing of the birds pretty nearly to perfection. He also imitated the meadowlarks, called the Sioux bird. He was said to understand what the meadowlarks say. He was particularly fond of the yellowhammer."

Sitting Bull's fondness for the yellowhammer was understandable. One day, tired from the hunt, he lay down under a tree for a nap. As he slept, he dreamed that a yellowhammer woodpecker had an eye on him from a nearby hollow tree trunk. Suddenly Sitting Bull heard the underbrush snap and break under the weight of a mighty animal that could only be a grizzly bear. The woodpecker tapped twice on the tree trunk.

"Lie still! Lie still!"

Against every instinct, Sitting Bull kept his eyes closed and lay motionless as death. The crashing sounds and the bear's loud snuffling drew closer, paused, and then continued on until they faded away. Sitting Bull opened his eyes to see the woodpecker still drumming on the tree trunk . . . and still watching him. The bird had saved his life. With hands held upward, Sitting Bull gave thanks to the woodpecker in song.

> *"Pretty bird you have seen me and took pity on me;*
> *Amongst the tribes to live, you wish for me.*
> *Ye Bird Tribes from henceforth, always my relation*
>   *shall be."*

Sitting Bull may have been a warrior, hunter, singer, and friend to all creatures, but he had a higher goal. He wanted to be a holy man like his cousin Black Moon so that he could be a spiritual advisor to his people, interpret dreams, and foretell the future. To become a holy man, Sitting Bull knew that he would have to undergo the torture of the Sun Dance. He had witnessed too many Sun Dances not to know what he was committing himself to. It didn't matter. He had made up his mind to take that important step, and that was what he would do.

Every year at the full moon of midsummer, the Sioux bands came together to renew friendships, eat, sing, dance, and talk. Most of all they came together for the Sun Dance celebration, which would assure the well-being of the people and the continuing abundance of the buffalo. When Sitting Bull was still in his twenties, he gathered with his Icira band in a large camp on the Little Missouri River. The time had come, he decided, to participate in the Sun Dance.

The people feasted, danced, and sang for the first four days of the Sun Dance ceremonies. During the next four days, Black Moon, known as the Intercessor, instructed and rehearsed Sitting Bull and the other Sun Dance candidates. The final four days were Holy Days, when the cottonwood tree that was to be the sacred Sun Dance pole was selected by four young men, cut down by four young women, painted, and raised in the Dance circle. A leafy shelter was built around the circle to provide shade for the spectators.

On the day of the Sun Dance itself, Sitting Bull, like the other dancers, was purified in a sweat bath. He entered a small wigwam that had been built with the opening facing east to greet the rising sun, as did every Sioux tipi. A pit had been dug in the floor and filled with red-hot stones.

With his clothes off and the wigwam flap closed, Sitting Bull sat in the sweat lodge smoking a sacred pipe while cold water was thrown on the heated stones. The sweat lodge was well named. Scalding steam billowed off the stones, raising the temperature so high that Sitting Bull's naked body was soon drenched in sweat.

Sitting Bull and the other candidates then dried themselves off with branches of wild sage, which was a symbol of cleanliness and purity. Next they had their faces and bodies painted. Barefoot, with their hair loose, each man dressed in a long white deerskin apron and placed a downy white eagle feather in his hair. Carrying the sacred pipe, Black Moon escorted the Sun Dancers into the Dance circle, where they smoked, sang, and danced before a painted buffalo skull. Mothers then presented their babies to have their ears pierced, just as Sitting Bull's ears had been pierced when he was an infant.

Knowing what was to come next, Sitting Bull surely must have had at least a fleeting moment of hesitation. Perhaps not. Perhaps he was able to keep his mind on being in communion with Wakan Tanka, the Great Mystery, from which all things came. Either way, he lay quietly on the ground as his seconder bent over him and cut two four-inch slits in his chest and back. After inserting pointed sticks in the slits, Sitting Bull's seconder lifted him to his feet and tied the sticks to rawhide thongs that hung from the crossbar of the Sun Dance pole.

On his feet and in excruciating pain, Sitting Bull gazed up at the blazing sun and blew on an eagle-bone whistle that hung around his neck. Forbidden to touch his body, he danced in place as he struggled to free himself as quickly as possible. Willing himself to ignore the pain, after about half an hour he yanked the sticks from his flesh in a burst of bright blood.

Even though medicine was applied to his wounds, Sitting Bull's ordeal wasn't over. He now had to stare up at the sun and continue to dance. Without food or water, he danced all that day, through the night, and into the next day. As he danced, he cried out to Wakan Tanka to give his people good health and food from the hunt.

Exhausted and in such intense pain that it finally became numbing, Sitting Bull heard the voice of Wakan Tanka promising to give him what he asked for. This was the goal that he had hoped to attain, communion with Wakan Tanka. From the depths of his sacrifice, he had received assurance that Wakan Tanka had heard his prayers and would provide for his people.

Strong and determined as Sitting Bull was, he could endure only so much, and on the second day he collapsed. Like the other dancers, he was lifted by loving hands into the shade and

23

given food and water. After Sitting Bull had been purified in a sweat bath, his family and friends gathered around to praise and care for him.

And so Sitting Bull was raised to the elite ranks of holy men. His adopted son One Bull later remarked, "Lots of times Sitting Bull took part in Sun Dance—he wanted to learn to love his god and his people."

Sitting Bull didn't need the Sun Dance to learn to love his people. He already did. "Be it small children, grown-ups, rich or poor—all alike, he has a heartfelt feeling towards them— loves them all," a fellow tribesman said.

There was no question that Sitting Bull embodied the four Sioux virtues: bravery, fortitude, generosity, and wisdom. But more than that, as he grew into manhood he attained an even higher level of virtue. The Hunkpapa Crow Dog described his unique gift: "To see with the eye in one's heart, rather than the eyes in one's head." Above all, Sitting Bull saw with the eyes in his heart.

◄ 6 ►

We did not make a blunder,
We rubbed out Little Thunder,
And we sent him to the other side of Jordan.

U.S. Army Song Celebrating
the Little Thunder Massacre

Because Sitting Bull and his Sioux tribe of three thousand Hunkpapas lived far to the north in what is now North and South Dakota and Montana, neither they nor their land were of much interest to the whites. Consequently, throughout the 1850s the Hunkpapas' main contact with the *Wasichus,* as they called the whites, was with traders.

For the most part, the Hunkpapas traded at Fort Pierre on the Missouri River, the run-down trading post which they called "Wornout Fences." There they traded buffalo robes and tanned hides for those goods which they had come to depend upon but couldn't make themselves: guns, ammunition, blankets, knives, iron pots, tools, glass beads, coffee, and tobacco.

At one time, Sitting Bull acted as a trade chief for a white trader, grading robes and hides. But Sitting Bull insisted that the trader give his people a fair exchange, which was definitely not what the trader had in mind. Finally, after two years, Sitting Bull quit in a dispute over his wages.

The Hunkpapas also traded with French Indians called Métis. Coming down from Canada, the Métis brought their trade goods in sleighs to the Hunkpapas' winter camps. During the rest of the year they transported their wares in long trains of squeaky, two-wheeled wooden carts. The Hunkpapas not only traded with the scrappy Métis, but occasionally skirmished with them as well.

Surprisingly enough, another source of white man's goods came from the United States government. In 1851 the government brought together ten thousand Plains Indians for a council at Birch Grove near Fort Laramie. Delegates from all the Plains tribes gathered in a huge encampment, friend and foe alike. In recognition of the largest assembly of Plains Indians ever to come together, 1851 was known in the Hunkpapa picture calendar as "Tribes-Gathered-at-Birch-Grove."

Although some Hunkpapas attended the council, Sitting Bull was too young to have been one of them. However, a number of tribal chiefs who were present touched the pen to a government treaty. After they touched the pen, white officials signed the chiefs' names. The terms of the treaty granted all the Plains peoples fifty thousand dollars' worth of rations and goods over a fifteen-year period. The annuities, as they were called, were to be distributed by white Indian agents, who were appointed by the Indian Bureau in Washington. The Sioux, who anticipated a windfall, called the treaty "The-Treaty-of-Plenty-Rations."

But they had been deceived. First of all, the rations weren't "plenty." Second, the chiefs who had touched the pen to the treaty hadn't understood all of its terms. Boundary lines were drawn for each tribe. They were not to fight their tribal enemies. They were to allow safe travel on the Oregon Trail. Roads and military posts could be built on Indian lands. On the other hand, the Indians were promised protection from any white aggression.

The treaty was broken all the way around. Not only did the Plains tribes continue to wage warfare on one another, but in 1854 fighting broke out between the Sioux and the soldiers stationed at Fort Laramie.

In 1849 gold had been discovered in California, and the Oregon Trail was opened as the fastest route west. But the Oregon Trail ran through prime Oglala and Brulé Sioux hunting grounds. Before long the steady stream of wagon trains had driven away the game and turned the rich grasslands into a dusty desert.

As angry young warriors harassed the wagon trains, resentment built on both sides. Finally, in a foolish argument over a stolen cow, thirty infantrymen marched from Fort Laramie into the nearby Sioux encampment. When they opened fire on a Brulé chieftain and his people, hundreds of enraged warriors charged out of hiding and killed all thirty soldiers.

In retaliation, General William Harney led his troops in a surprise attack on a Brulé village not far from Fort Laramie that was headed by Chief Little Thunder. After killing eighty-six men, women, and children, Harney, known to the Sioux as White Beard, marched seventy Brulé captives to Fort Laramie for imprisonment. From there he and his command made their way through the heart of Sioux lands to the Missouri River. Stunned by the slaughter of Little Thunder's village, no warrior raised a hand against them. For the first time, blue-coated soldiers were a presence deep in Hunkpapa territory, prompting the Hunkpapas to record the year 1855 in their picture calendar as "White-Beard-Hinders-the-Sioux."

In March of the following year, White Beard Harney summoned Sioux headmen to a council at Fort Pierre, where he and his troops had set up winter headquarters. Sitting Bull's uncle Chief Four Horns was there, and Sitting Bull, now twenty-five, probably was too. His first experience with a soldier chief must have been an eye-opener. Right away White Beard appointed a head chief for each tribe. That a *Wasichu* had the arrogance to interfere in Sioux tribal matters was astounding, not only to Sitting Bull but to all the other chiefs as well.

Much to Sitting Bull's displeasure, White Beard named Bear's Rib chief of all the Hunkpapas. Unlike Sitting Bull, Bear's Rib favored peace with both tribal enemies and the *Wasichus*. Soon after the council was over, White Beard and his men abandoned Fort Pierre, leaving behind the "paper chief" Bear's Rib and bad memories.

Because he continued to control the yearly handing out of government annuities, Bear's Rib was able to hold on to his chieftainship. But by the 1860s, the Hunkpapas, like the Oglalas and Brulés to the south, were paying dearly for their rations and gifts. *Wasichus* were increasingly trespassing on their hunting grounds, scattering the buffalo and ruining the rich grasses that their pony herds and game depended on. Although a decision had to be made as to what should be done, the Hunkpapas had divided into two quarreling factions.

The peace party, led by Bear's Rib, urged peace with everyone. Sitting Bull and the other young warriors spearheaded the war party. Fed up with talk of peace, they yearned for the prestige that only warfare could bring. Furthermore, they wanted nothing to do with either the white man's goods or the Indian agents who scolded them for not living up to a treaty that they had never signed.

In June of 1862, two young warriors shot and killed Bear's Rib. With Bear's Rib dead, Sitting Bull and his war party took over the reins of power. "We notified the Bear's Rib yearly not to receive your goods; he had no ears, and we gave him ears by killing him," ten Hunkpapa chiefs wrote to the Indian agent. "We also say to you that we wish you to stop the whites from travelling through our country, and if you do not stop them, we will. If your whites have no ears we will give them ears."

Although the *Wasichus* had received a fair warning to stay off Hunkpapa lands, they ignored it. Gold had been discovered in Montana, and the rush was on. Gold prospectors traveled by "fire-boat," or steamboat, up the Missouri River or by foot across the Hunkpapas' hunting grounds. In the summer of 1862 enraged Hunkpapa warriors attacked a Missouri River fire-boat that was filled with white miners.

During that same summer, the Hunkpapas' Dakota Sioux cousins to the east in Minnesota rose up in a bloody rebellion that left hundreds of white settlers and soldiers dead. Life for the three divisions of the Sioux Nation would never be the same again.

It wouldn't be the same for that division known as the Dakota Sioux, who lived in Minnesota and eastern Dakota.

It wouldn't be the same for the Yankton and Yanktonais Sioux, who lived in the Missouri River Valley.

It wouldn't even be the same for the three thousand Teton Sioux who rode the Great Plains as buffalo hunters west of the Missouri River. The seven tribes of the Teton Sioux were the Hunkpapas, Oglalas, Brulés, Miniconjous, Blackfeet-Sioux, Sans Arcs, and Two Kettles. Although the proper name for these Teton Sioux was Lakota, over the years they have traditionally been called Sioux.

By 1862, the Dakotas and the Army were at war in Minnesota, but it wasn't until July 1863 that fighting broke out between the Hunkpapas and the Army. Led by Sitting Bull, a large party of Hunkpapas and Blackfeet-Sioux were hunting buffalo just east of the Missouri River when they unexpectedly met up with General Henry Sibley and his troops. Sibley, who had been in charge of putting down the Dakota uprising in Minnesota the year before, was out searching for any Dakotas who might have escaped his grasp.

With the arrival of the very Dakotas whom Sibley and his cavalrymen were looking for, Sitting Bull's party swelled to sixteen hundred warriors. Their original intention had been to hunt buffalo. Now all that was changed. With his formidable force, Sitting Bull was confident that he could easily whip these pony soldiers who were so brazenly trespassing on Sioux lands.

Leading the attack on Sibley and his troops at Dead Buffalo

Lake, Sitting Bull, as usual, broke ranks first. On his warhorse Bloated Jaw, he galloped down the hill amid flying bullets. Triumphantly he counted coup on a mule herder and made off with an Army mule. But long-distance firing from small cannons mounted on wheels, called howitzers, caught Sitting Bull and his war party by surprise. Before they could inflict any real damage, the heavy artillery forced them to withdraw.

Although Sibley and his forces followed the warriors' trail to Stony Lake twenty-one miles away, Sitting Bull was far from giving up. He was determined to defeat these pony soldiers, who were called Long Knives because of the deadly, mutilating sabers they carried.

On July 28, two days after their first encounter, Sitting Bull and his war party launched another strike. Riding down in a five-mile-long line, they split in the center, flanking the troops on either side in order to get at the baggage train in the rear. But once again, the Long Knives' howitzers drove them off. In retreat the warriors crossed the Missouri River, where they gathered along the west bank, defiantly flashing their hand mirrors at the Long Knives.

Sitting Bull had no desire to fight these blue-coated soldiers. He much preferred to fight the Crows and Hohes. Stealing horses and taking scalps was what real warfare was all about. But here the Long Knives were, marching all over the countryside, firing their far-shooting guns, trampling the grasses, cutting down already scarce timber, and frightening off the game. The *Wasichus* had been told to leave but they had refused to listen. Well then, it was up to him, Sitting Bull, head Hunkpapa war chief, to see that they were given ears.

◄ 7 ►

Tremble, O Tribe of the Enemy
This earth I had used as paint
Causes the tribe of the enemy much excitement.

Hunkpapa War Paint Song

Sitting Bull wasn't discouraged by his two defeats at the hands of Sibley and his Long Knives in the summer of 1863. Far from it. Stubbornly determined as always, he was itching to fight them again. And he wholeheartedly stood behind the challenge that the Hunkpapa chiefs had thrown out to the Army: "All we ask of you is to bring men, and not women dressed in soldiers' clothes." This time victory would be theirs.

Sitting Bull wasn't the only one who wanted to prove himself. By the end of July 1864, fourteen hundred lodges of Hunkpapas, Blackfeet-Sioux, Miniconjous, Yanktonai, and Dakotas had joined forces to take on these "women dressed in soldiers' clothes." They gathered in a four-mile-long encampment near a favorite Sioux hunting ground "at the place where they killed the deer," or Killdeer Mountain.

Scouts, known as wolves, briefed Sitting Bull, Inkpaduta, who had been the Dakota leader of the Minnesota uprising, and the other war chiefs on Army movements. During the daylight hours they signaled by flashing hand mirrors in the sun. At night they shot fire arrows into the sky. "The soldiers are coming near and will be here tomorrow," the scouts reported on July 27.

On a hot and dusty July 28, 1864, more than two thousand infantry- and cavalrymen under General Alfred Sully marched down from the hills and headed toward the Sioux village. It was just what Sitting Bull had been hoping for. The rocky terrain, with its bluffs and timber-lined ravines, was no problem for the warriors' small, sturdy ponies, but was almost impassable for the big American horses.

And Sully was the soldier-chief Sitting Bull was most eager to fight. Only weeks before, three Dakotas who had killed an Army officer had been captured and executed. On Sully's orders their heads had been set on poles high on a hill to serve as a gruesome warning to their fellow tribesmen.

With great anticipation, Sitting Bull, his uncle Chief Four Horns, and his sister Good Feather's oldest son, White Bull, who was fourteen, dressed and painted for battle. Trailing their trained warhorses behind them, the colorful war party of some two thousand men rode out to meet the enemy. Sitting Bull and the other war chiefs were so sure of success that they didn't even direct the women to pack up their tipis and belongings in case they had to flee. Instead, the women, children, and old ones climbed a high hill in great excitement to cheer on a Sioux victory.

But when the war party was five miles out, Sitting Bull and his warriors were startled to see that the Long Knives had dismounted and were on foot, their curving sabers gleaming in the bright July sun. The war party quickly gathered on every hillock and bluff as the Long Knives marched toward them. As they drew near, the warrior Lone Dog stepped forward.

"Let me go close and if they shoot at me we will then all shoot at the soldiers," he proposed. That way the Long Knives would be the first to fire. Sitting Bull agreed.

As soon as Lone Dog rode out, shouting and waving his war club, the soldiers opened fire. The battle was on. Lone Dog's stunt had worked, and he hadn't been hit. But then no one had expected him to be. White Bull explained that Lone Dog "was with a ghost and it was hard to shoot at him—he had a charm."

Although the two forces were about even, the odds turned out to be hopelessly uneven. The warriors fought as they always had. With every man for himself, they circled, darted in, fired off arrows or a few rounds, and then withdrew. Sometimes they joined forces for a quick hit-and-run attack, but their bows, arrows, lances, tomahawks, war clubs, muskets, and outdated rifles were no match for the cavalry's six-shooters, long-range rifles, and howitzers. Drawing their dreaded sabers, a Minnnesota battalion, hot for revenge, charged Inkpaduta's Dakotas and engaged them in vicious hand-to-hand combat.

The Long Knives were soon pushing the warriors back, back, back, toward their encampment. Displaying his usual courage and daring, Sitting Bull fought desperately to hold the line, but by evening the troops were drawing perilously close to the tipi circles. Suddenly Sitting Bull heard his uncle cry out, "I am shot!"

Quickly wheeling Bloated Jaw to Four Horns's side, Sitting Bull grabbed the bridle of his uncle's horse. Accompanied by White Bull, he led the injured man from the battlefield. As might be expected of a chief whose first concern was always his people's welfare, Sitting Bull carried medicine with him at all times. But while he was dressing and bandaging Four Horns's wound, the Long Knives overran the Sioux village. With the warriors fighting valiantly to cover their escape, the terrified women and children fled to safety in the mountains. In their haste, they had to leave behind their tipis, belongings, and all the food that they had stored for the winter. The Long Knives torched everything.

Sitting Bull and the rest of his war party were stunned by their disastrous defeat at the Battle of Killdeer Mountain. At least Four Horns, who said that he could feel the bullet inside him, survived. But some forty warriors didn't survive, a terrible loss that set the people to wailing and cutting their arms and legs in mourning. Although the Army later claimed that they had killed at least one hundred warriors, Sitting Bull's old friend Gall disputed that figure. One hundred or forty, either number was too many.

No war chief, especially Sitting Bull, was willing to accept such a defeat, and he resolved to engage the Long Knives again. This time he would wipe them out. From Killdeer Mountain, the whole village packed up what had been saved from the fire and traveled to the western edge of the Dakota Badlands, not far from the Little Missouri River. There, more

35

Miniconjous, Brulés, Sans Arcs, and even some Northern Cheyennes joined them.

Scouts kept track of Sully and his Long Knives as they traveled through the Badlands. Eroded by rain, wind, and the Little Missouri River, the Badlands were all gloomy gorges, rounded hillocks of many colors, buttes, canyons, cliffs, and deep twisting ravines, with boulders scattered over dry riverbeds as if thrown from the sky. Sitting Bull and his men, who knew this desolate country well, called it *Mako shika,* meaning "no-good land." It was, however, ideal for the ambush warfare that they favored. It was also in the war party's favor that Sully and his Long Knives had to travel at a snail's pace with their heavy artillery and wagon trains.

Wild to get at the Long Knives, Sitting Bull rallied his warriors. "Saddle up; saddle up!" he cried as soon as they had painted themselves and their horses. "We are going to fight the soldiers again."

Using the terrain to their advantage, thousands of Sioux and Cheyenne warriors positioned themselves in hidden ravines and crevasses. Keeping up a constant harassment of the Long Knives, the warriors surprised an advance party here or a rear guard there. But it wasn't enough. Once again bursting howitzer shells inflicted casualties and kept the war party at a distance.

Sitting Bull had wanted this fight badly, but he was losing heart. They were low on ammunition, and their weapons were doing little damage. Furthermore, all their food supplies had been destroyed at Killdeer Mountain, and his people were hungry.

"Let them go and we will go home," he called out.

There would be no shame in retreating. As soon as a battle looked hopeless, it made sense to pull back before more warriors were killed or wounded. On the other hand, just because Sitting Bull was Hunkpapa war chief didn't mean that he had to be obeyed. Warriors were always free to fight or not as they chose, and on this occasion they chose to fight. No matter how strongly Sitting Bull may have felt about withdrawing, he stayed on with his men.

In the middle of the third night, a voice shouted out from the darkness, "We are about thirsty to death and want to know what Indians are you?" It was one of General Sully's Winnebago scouts.

"Hunkpapas, Sans Arcs, Yanktonais, and others," Sitting Bull shouted back. "Who are you?"

"Some Indians with soldiers," came the Winnebago's reply. "Most white boys are starved and thirsty to death so just stay around and they will be dead."

Sitting Bull knew that the Sioux' enemies often served as Army scouts, and it made his heart bad. "You have no business with the soldiers," he yelled. "The Indians here want no fight with the whites." Then he asked the question that was puzzling him. "Why is it the whites come to fight with the Indians?"

The Winnebago scout had no answer for that. Perhaps he, too, was puzzled. The Plains tribes fought for prestige, horses, and to protect their people, not to acquire land. Land couldn't be owned any more than the sky could be owned.

Finally, on the afternoon of August 9, 1864, the Sioux and Cheyennes gave up and withdrew, just as Sitting Bull had urged them to do three days before. And with their withdrawal, the great camp broke up. Sitting Bull and some one hundred Hunkpapas drifted to the southeast on the trail of a buffalo herd. But instead of buffalo, they picked up the trail of a hundred wagons filled with miners headed for the Montana goldfields. Fifty Long Knives escorted them.

Sitting Bull knew that if they were patient they could pick off this prey easily. Just as a pack of wolves stalks an elk herd, Sitting Bull and his party stalked the wagon train. And then, on September 2, one of the wagons overturned on its way down a steep ravine. A second wagon stopped to help.

It was just what Sitting Bull had been waiting for. Whooping and hollering, he led his men in a headlong charge, reaching the scene first on Bloated Jaw. But as he tried to wrestle a soldier off his big horse, the soldier grabbed his revolver and shot at close range. The bullet tore into Sitting Bull's left hip and out the small of his back. Despite the agonizing pain, he didn't faint or even cry out. Instead, he managed to slip down on the far side of Bloated Jaw and ride out of firing range.

White Bull, who called Sitting Bull's feat one of his bravest stunts, was instantly at his uncle's side. Sitting Bull's adopted brother, Jumping Bull, now twenty, and a third warrior rode quickly over to assist. Steadying Sitting Bull on Bloated Jaw, they led him away from the scene of the fighting. After they eased him to the ground, Jumping Bull tended to the wound with medicine that he had with him. The three men then accompanied Sitting Bull the seven miles back to camp. Although they may have been disappointed to leave what promised to be a victorious fight, caring for a wounded comrade came first.

As Sitting Bull recuperated from the bullet wound that gave the battle the name "Sitting Bull Wounded," he had time to think. And he thought about the blue-coated Long Knives. Much about them was perplexing.

"They seem to have no hearts," he observed. "When an Indian gets killed, the other Indians feel sorry and cry, and sometimes stop fighting. But when a white soldier gets killed, nobody cries, nobody cares. They go right on shooting and let him lie there. Sometimes they even go off and leave their wounded behind them."

When his uncle Four Horns had been wounded at Killdeer Mountain, Sitting Bull hadn't hesitated. Even though he was war chief, he had left the battlefield to tend to his uncle. Now White Bull and Jumping Bull had done the same for him. With concern and heart, that was how he and his warriors fought.

◀ 8 ▶

Father has advised me by words
So the weak ones
I have been helping.

Hunkpapa Song of Helping

Even though Sitting Bull's hip wound put him out of the action, his warriors carried on without him. Because their attack had caught the wagon train by surprise, they were able to fight at close range in the hand-to-hand combat at which they excelled. They kept up the pressure in a three-day running battle until the Long Knives corraled the wagons into a well-fortified circle and built a breastwork of sod. Although the warriors killed eight Long Knives and a number of miners, the *Wasichus* were able to hold them at bay from their little fortification for fourteen days. Finally, the war party lost interest and rode off to hunt buffalo.

Sitting Bull's bullet wound was both serious and painful, and he immediately put himself in the hands of a medicine man. But his recovery was slow. He could tolerate the pain; it was being so helpless that he found hard to accept. Accustomed to the winged hooves of Bloated Jaw, an unhappy Sitting Bull was transported everywhere in a willow basket for the next three months. The willow basket was lashed to two long poles, which were fastened to a horse's bridle to make a travois. At least he wasn't totally idle. His famous peacemaking skills turned out to be needed badly in camp.

A white woman, Fanny Kelly, had been captured in July by some Oglalas and traded to the Hunkpapa warrior Brings Plenty. Although a gift of horses had been offered for her safe return, Brings Plenty wasn't interested. He considered Real Woman, as he called her, to be his wife and he was well pleased with the arrangement. Brings Plenty may have been pleased, but Sitting Bull could plainly see that Fanny Kelly was not. Of all the seven Sioux tribes, the Hunkpapas were the most quarrelsome, and Fanny Kelly's presence in camp was causing jealousy and friction.

Sitting Bull sought to restore peace. "Friends, this woman is out of our way. Her ways are different," he pointed out diplomatically. "I can see in her face that she is homesick and so I am sending her back."

But Brings Plenty wouldn't hear of it. Twice Sitting Bull urged Brings Plenty to let Fanny Kelly return to her people, and twice Brings Plenty refused. Finally, accompanied by his friend Crawler, Sitting Bull approached Brings Plenty in his tipi. Forcing himself to stand straight and tall in spite of his wound, he spoke with the authority of head Hunkpapa war chief.

"My friend, I sent for this woman to be brought to me at my tipi and you would not give her up," he scolded.

Pulling rank did the trick. When Crawler motioned to Fanny

Kelly to come stand by Sitting Bull, Brings Plenty didn't dare object. With no further discussion, the three of them left.

Later Sitting Bull directed Crawler and several other Strong Heart warriors to escort Fanny Kelly safely back to her husband. Sitting Bull had seen beyond Fanny Kelly's white skin and pale eyes and sympathized with her misery. He had looked at her with the eyes in his heart rather than the eyes in his head. His wisdom in solving the thorny situation and his generosity toward the white captive moved the Hunkpapas to call 1864 in their picture calendar "The-Winter-When-the-White-Woman-Was-Rescued."

◄ 9 ►

Friends, I am a soldier
And have many people
Jealous of me!

Sitting Bull's War Song

Sitting Bull had felt sympathy for the white woman but he felt nothing but outrage toward the miners, settlers, and Long Knives who were overrunning Hunkpapa hunting grounds. He would rather not have dealt with white traders, either, but he and his people didn't have much choice. Their only source of white man's goods, especially firearms and ammunition, was still at the three trading posts on the Missouri River: Fort Pierre, Fort Berthold, and Fort Union.

But Sitting Bull had become wary. The Missouri River, which the Hunkpapas called The Furious because of its swift, wild currents, was acquiring an ominous new look. Military forts were going up all along its banks. Fort Randall on the Dakota and Nebraska border had been the first, built by White Beard Harney in 1856, the year after the Little Thunder massacre. Seven years later the Army put up Fort Sully only twenty miles north of the Fort Pierre trading post. Sitting Bull was even more alarmed when Fort Rice was built the following summer. Going up on the west bank of the Missouri River, Fort Rice pierced more than one hundred miles deeper into Hunkpapa country than Fort Sully.

As if the forts weren't troublesome enough, in October 1864, General Alfred Sully called all the Hunkpapas and Blackfeet-Sioux to a council at Fort Sully. The only ones the least bit interested were those "friendlies," such as Bear Rib's son, who declared that they had been foolish to fight the whites. All they wanted was peace.

After having been routed twice in clashes with Sully, Sitting Bull most definitely was not interested in attending. Instead, as soon as the new growth of rich grasses fattened up the ponies in the spring of 1865, he organized raids on Fort Rice.

At first Sitting Bull and his warriors limited themselves to striking the fort's woodcutting parties and livestock herds. And then on July 28, 1865, Sitting Bull led three hundred Hunkpapas, Blackfeet-Sioux, and Sans Arcs in an attack on the fort itself. At the peak of his powers as a warrior, he was an impressive figure. He had painted his body and face red and wore "a headdress of feathers and plumes that fell half way over his back."

In his favorite role as fronter, Sitting Bull galloped into action on Bloated Jaw ahead of the others, with war whoops and shouts. But after stealing two Army horses, he suddenly left the field with no explanation. It may have been that his hip wound still bothered him. Or it may have been that he felt his medi-

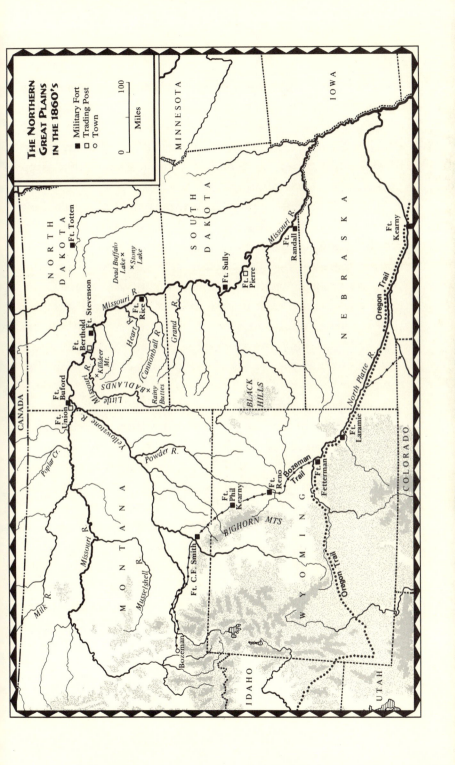

THE NORTHERN
GREAT PLAINS
IN THE 1860's

■ Military Fort
□ Trading Post
○ Town

0   100
Miles

CANADA

NORTH DAKOTA

■ Ft. Totten

Deau Buffalo Lake ×   × Stony Lake

SOUTH DAKOTA

MINNESOTA

IOWA

Missouri R.

■ Ft. Stevenson

Ft. Berthold □

Missouri R.

Ft. Rice ■
Heart R.

Ft. Buford

Ft. Union □

Killdeer Mt. ×

BADLANDS

Rainy Buttes ×

Cannonball R.

Grand R.

■ Ft. Sully

Ft. Pierre □

Missouri R.

Ft. Randall ■

NEBRASKA

Ft. Kearny ■

Little Missouri R.

Poplar Cr.

Yellowstone R.

BLACK HILLS

Powder R.

North Platte R.

Oregon Trail

MONTANA

Milk R.

Missouri R.

Musselshell R.

Ft. C.F. Smith ■

Ft. Phil Kearny ■

BIGHORN MTS

Ft. Reno ■

Bozeman Trail

Ft. Fetterman ■

Ft. Laramie ■

COLORADO

WYOMING

IDAHO

Bozeman

Oregon Trail

UTAH

cine, or power, was weak that day. Whatever the reason, the rest of the warriors continued to fight courageously until long-range military weapons forced them to withdraw.

Later, back in camp, the warriors, who complained about Sitting Bull's abrupt leave-taking, killed his two stolen Army horses, or so it was rumored.

Even without Sitting Bull, the war party had conveyed their message. Sully could hold all the peace talks that he wanted, but they were going to continue fighting. The *Wasichus* apparently weren't all that interested in peace anyway. Soon after their attack on Fort Rice, Sitting Bull, the Hunkpapas, and their allies headed west toward the Powder River. By chance they happened upon some two thousand blue-coated soldiers who had been marching around the Powder River country for weeks searching for "savages" to fight. Instead, the "savages" found them.

As two young warriors approached the walking soldiers to ask for some tobacco, the soldiers opened fire. When the warriors told Sitting Bull that the soldiers had fired first, he was furious.

"Brace up! Brace up! We'll get them yet!" he shouted to his men as they prepared for battle.

Riding down into the Powder River valley at the head of four hundred warriors, Sitting Bull led his war party in a charge on the troops. For three days they kept up a steady barrage of hit-and-run strikes until September 5, 1865, when they launched a united attack. But Sitting Bull, who was painted for war and wearing two feathers in his hair, was once again more concerned with stealing a couple of Army horses than he was in fighting. Other warriors, especially Bull Head, won the war honors of the day.

With the Long Knives' supplies low and many of their horses and pack mules lost, the exhausted and starving troops were close to collapse. Yet Sitting Bull and his war party abandoned the fight. For them winning a battle was victory enough, and they didn't see any sense in pursuing a defeated enemy when it might result in more casualties.

By 1866, the *Wasichus* had pockmarked the open plains with still more forts. The Army had occupied Fort Laramie to the southwest since 1849. Now a new road called the Bozeman Trail, which began at Fort Laramie, cut through Oglala Sioux hunting grounds to the goldfields of Montana. To protect white travelers, the Army built three new forts along the route, Fort Reno, Fort Phil Kearny, and Fort C. F. Smith.

Forts were also closing in on the Hunkpapas to the north. Sitting Bull was enraged to see another military fort, Fort Buford, go up where the Yellowstone River flowed into the wide Missouri River. Only two miles from the Fort Union trading post, Fort Buford violated the very heart of Hunkpapa hunting grounds, and Sitting Bull hated Fort Buford above all others.

Pouring all his energies into heading raids against Fort Buford, Sitting Bull led an attack on the fort across the frozen Missouri River on December 23, 1866. After his warriors captured the Army icehouse and sawmill, they kept up a steady firing at the stockade itself. Despite his war fever, Sitting Bull hadn't lost his sense of humor. In high good spirits at their victory, he beat musical time on the sawmill's large circular saw blade and accompanied himself in song.

"Friends, I am a soldier
And have many people
Jealous of me!"

Sitting Bull's war party managed to set fire to Fort Buford's entire supply of winter firewood the next day. But once again the military's cannons forced them back. Long-range guns! Fighting the *Wasichus* always seemed to come down to being driven off by their long-range guns.

Over to the west, the Hunkpapas' Oglala cousins were experiencing more success. Chief Red Cloud, Crazy Horse, and their war parties managed to halt all traffic on the Bozeman Trail. On a bitterly cold December day they wiped out a whole column of Long Knives at Fort Phil Kearny in what they called "The-Hundred-Soldiers-Killed Fight."

That winter the Great Plains was held in the grip of the worst weather in anyone's memory. Two-foot-deep snowstorms were followed by hail and then a steady rain that froze solid, turning the countryside into a treacherous ice field. With snowblindness common and their ponies without forage, the Hunkpapas named 1867 "Icy-Winter" in their picture calendar.

Despite the blizzards and cold, Sitting Bull and his warriors kept up their offensive on Fort Buford. All through the frigid Plains winter they struck, and struck hard. By the time spring arrived, they had cut the fort off from all communication with the outside world.

But the Army didn't fight just battles. The Army fought wars, and when defeat seemed close at hand, the United States government propped up the military with more men, weapons, and fortifications. In 1867 the Army was ordered to construct Fort Stevenson on the upper Missouri River, just a few miles from the Fort Berthold trading post. All three Missouri River trading posts were now hemmed in by Army forts.

During that same year, Fort Totten went up some one hundred miles east of Fort Stevenson, with a mail route linking the two. While Sitting Bull spent most of the summer in the north attacking Fort Buford, his Hunkpapa patrols harassed Fort Stevenson. If any unfortunate mail carriers happened to get in the way, they were picked off too.

Now more than ever, the Hunkpapas needed guns and ammunition. The military forts were forbidden to trade firearms with the Sioux, but the Army had no control over the trading posts. Sitting Bull and his Hunkpapas continued to trade robes and hides for guns and ammunition at the trading posts, mostly at Fort Berthold. To keep their distance from the despised soldiers at nearby Fort Stevenson, they set up their tipis ten miles away on the opposite bank of the Missouri River. Bringing their goods across the river by boat, the traders bargained with the Hunkpapas in a special trading lodge.

If Sitting Bull needed proof that these blue-coated *Wasichus* weren't about to go away, by 1868 he had it. The many thousands of square miles of Sioux land were now completely ringed by military forts. In a buffalo surround, the hunters always approached downwind, encircling the herd before the buffalo were aware of the danger. Now it was the Sioux themselves who were encircled in a surround. But like the courageous and stubborn buffalo bull, Sitting Bull wasn't about to give up. The headstrong child Slow had become the determined war chief Sitting Bull.

"I have killed, robbed, and injured too many whites," he acknowledged. "They are medicine and I would eventually die a lingering death. I had rather die on the field of battle."

◄ 10 ►

Going on the warpath
You should give up and settle down
You should desire
And stop for good.

A Mother's Song to Her Son

Sometime after the death of his first wife, Sitting Bull married two women, Snow-on-Her, with whom he had two daughters, and Red Woman, with whom he had a son. Taking two wives, or more, wasn't out of the ordinary, especially for a man of Sitting Bull's high rank. Although the first to marry was wife-in-charge, the companionship of sharing the day-to-day chores proved to be a happy arrangement for most women.

Not so for Sitting Bull's wives, who argued and bickered constantly. An old friend described Sitting Bull as a peace-loving man: "Sitting Bull never wants trouble. Sitting Bull always wants peace." It was true. Sitting Bull especially wanted peace and harmony in his own tipi. It was not to be.

Finally he couldn't take any more quarreling. Realizing that Snow-on-Her was the troublemaker, he divorced her by "beating the drum" and announcing that their marriage was over. As for their two daughters, there was no question as to who would raise them. He would.

Much to Sitting Bull's sorrow, only a few years later, Red Woman fell ill and died. Still a young man, Sitting Bull had lost two wives and a son. Heartsick, he once again went into mourning, along with Red Woman's relatives and the rest of his village. As he slowly recovered from his grief, he faced the responsibility of raising three small children alone. Calling on his sister Good Feather to help, he brought her into his tipi.

Sitting Bull's widowed mother, Her-Holy-Door, was already living in the family tipi. Sioux women raised their daughters until they were married and sons until their teen years. Although Sitting Bull was well past his teen years, Her-Holy-Door didn't hesitate to give him plenty of advice. He was in his thirties now, an age when most warriors began to ease up on their fighting. Her-Holy-Door, who was a wise and good-natured woman, urged him to be more cautious. After all, he had been wounded three times, walked with a permanent limp, and was responsible for his three children, and his adopted son, One Bull, not to mention his sister and herself.

"You must hang back in war time," she counseled him. "Try and use a little judgment. Be careful."

Although Sitting Bull respected and loved his mother dearly, that was one bit of advice that he chose to ignore. He had, in fact, composed a song that must have especially annoyed her. With his waggish sense of humor, he may even have sung it to tease her.

No chance for me to live!
Mother, you might as well mourn.

Although Her-Holy-Door probably didn't find that particular song amusing, like her son she was warmhearted, and Sitting Bull's tipi was usually filled with laughter. "When Sitting Bull was in his own teepee he often joked with others," One Bull recalled.

Robert Higheagle agreed. "Sitting Bull could take a joke on himself. I have been in Sitting Bull's lodge many times and listened to the people cracking jokes," he said. "They were free to talk to each other in any manner."

There may have been laughter and good talk, but as time went on, Sitting Bull realized that his children badly needed a mother . . . and he needed a wife. Because he was attracted to Four Robes, he offered some of his finest horses to her brother Gray Eagle. Sitting Bull's horses were the best. "Sitting Bull liked horses and had many; liked white and greys," a family member said. "Sitting Bull had wonderful fast horses. When out camping Sitting Bull's horses [were] as noted as he, for speed."

When Gray Eagle gave his approval by accepting the gift of horses, Sitting Bull and Four Robes were married. A month or so later Four Robes's widowed sister, Seen-by-the-Nation, complained to Four Robes that she was lonely and wanted to marry Sitting Bull, too. It wasn't unusual for a man to marry two sisters because they tended to get along well. Sitting Bull, who obviously liked the idea, offered Gray Eagle his celebrated warhorse, Bloated Jaw, for Seen-by-the-Nation's hand.

It was an impressive gift. Sitting Bull had stolen Bloated Jaw from a white man years before and had ridden him into battle ever since. Needless to say, Gray Eagle promptly approved of the marriage. Gray Eagle described both of his sisters as "very respectable—very kind to everybody. Both jolly—never jealous."

When Seen-by-the-Nation moved into Sitting Bull's tipi, she brought two sons with her, Blue Mountain, who was deaf and mute, and Little Soldier. Sitting Bull settled in happily with his two cheerful wives, a pleasant change from his last experience of marrying two women. And if Sitting Bull ever regretted the loss of Bloated Jaw, he never mentioned it.

More than just family members were welcomed into Sitting Bull's tipi. On a bitterly cold January day in 1868, a young man, Frank Grouard, was making his way through a raging Plains blizzard when he was set upon by three Hunkpapa warriors. One pulled him from his horse, another tried to take his buffalo coat, and a third grabbed his pistol. As Grouard struggled for his life, a fourth warrior rode up.

"Let him go, let him go!" the fourth man ordered.

It was Sitting Bull. He had noticed the young man's swarthy complexion and long black hair and believed him to be an Indian. Quickly dismounting, Sitting Bull swung his bow and knocked Grouard's would-be killer to the ground. Immediately, the other warriors backed off, too. After speaking sharply to his men, Sitting Bull invited Grouard to join him in a friendly smoke.

When Sitting Bull returned to camp with the twenty-year-old Grouard, the warriors Gall and No Neck wanted to kill the stranger. But Sitting Bull had taken a liking to the young man, whose father was a white missionary and whose mother was Polynesian.

"It is my will that the captive shall not die," Sitting Bull announced. Besides, he pointed out, everyone had wanted to kill his adopted brother, Jumping Bull, and look at what a fine warrior he turned out to be.

Gall and No Neck couldn't argue with that, and shortly afterward, Sitting Bull took Grouard into his tipi and adopted him as a brother. Although Grouard was given the name Standing Bear, he was usually called the Grabber, a word that described how bears will often reach out and grab a victim in a "bear hug."

Sitting Bull was eager for his family to accept the newcomer. "These are my relatives. You are to call them as I do," he told the Grabber. "Just treat them fair and you will get along with them alright."

Fortunately, Sitting Bull's tipi was the largest one in camp. It was twelve feet in diameter, with four buffalo robes needed to cover the floor. Although all the space was taken, a full and lively tipi suited Sitting Bull just fine. No matter how badly warfare with the *Wasichus* might be going, he could always count on coming home to a warm and welcoming family circle.

‹ **11** ›

Whatever the tribe decide upon in council
That is what I wish to do my part in accomplishing.

Hunkpapa Council Song

In the spring of 1868 Sitting Bull received word that an important visitor was on his way. A Catholic priest, Father Pierre-Jean De Smet, known as the Black Robe, was traveling to Hunkpapa country. Sitting Bull had heard that the Black Robe was coming with a peace message. What he hadn't heard was that Father De Smet had been sent by the Indian office to try and convince the Hunkpapas to touch the pen to a new treaty.

To get his own message across, the month before the Black Robe was due to arrive, Sitting Bull headed war parties in hit-and-run raids on the three northern military forts: Buford, Stevenson, and Totten. They cut down Army patrols, stole livestock, and ambushed any whites caught out alone.

The raids didn't mean that Sitting Bull wouldn't greet the Black Robe with the greatest respect. He even planned to have

56

the priest stay with him and his family in their full-to-overflowing tipi. Nobody wanted peace more than Sitting Bull, and he knew that the Black Robe sincerely loved the Plains people and had traveled fearlessly among them for years. The Black Robe had not only urged them to keep the peace, but he had also done his best to convert them to Christianity.

When the Black Robe arrived after a long trip from Fort Rice, it was Sun Dance time. Sitting Bull and his Hunkpapas were camped with thousands of Sans Arcs, Blackfeet-Sioux, and Miniconjous on the Yellowstone River, near the mouth of the Powder River. The Powder River, which was wide and sandy, joined the Yellowstone in a great waterfall that roared like the roll of distant thunder.

Sitting Bull, his uncle Four Horns, his cousin Black Moon, and more than four hundred war-painted warriors in their most brilliant finery rode out ten miles to meet the Black Robe. At first, Sitting Bull and the other chiefs were startled by the sight of a strange flag flying from the Black Robe's carriage. But when they were reassured that it was a religious flag and not the American flag, they greeted their guest warmly. As the chiefs shook his hand one by one, the mounted warriors shouted and sang songs of welcome.

After accompanying the Black Robe back to camp, Sitting Bull made certain that *akicita* guards kept careful watch on his guest as he rested. He didn't dare take any chances. Some Hunkpapas, like the war chief White Gut, hated all *Wasichus*, no matter how honest and sincere they were.

"Here comes another white man to cheat us," was White Gut's angry reaction to the arrival of the Black Robe.

The Great Council was held on June 20, 1868, in a huge lodge that was made up of ten tipis. Escorted to the council lodge by the *akicita*, the Black Robe and his interpreters sat on buffalo robes facing the Hunkpapas' spiritual leader, Black Moon, and their political leader, Four Horns. Seated directly behind them were Sitting Bull and the lesser war chiefs: Gall, White Gut, and No Neck, while some five hundred warriors filled the rest of the lodge. The old men, women, and children gathered around the edges, craning their necks so as not to miss anything.

After an hour of singing, dancing, and the ceremonial smoking of the peace pipe, Black Moon welcomed the priest: "Speak, Black-robe, my ears are open to hear your words."

De Smet began his speech by urging the Sioux to meet with white officials at Fort Rice to sign the new Fort Laramie Treaty, which many of their Oglala and Brulé brethren had already signed.

The new treaty offered the Sioux fair terms, he declared. The Army would abandon their three forts along the Bozeman Trail that Crazy Horse and Red Cloud had fought against for so long. Boundaries would be drawn for a reservation, some twenty million acres, on which the seven Teton Sioux tribes would live. Called the Great Sioux Reservation, it would include all that land west of the Missouri River that would one day be part of South Dakota. No whites would ever be allowed "to pass over, settle upon, or reside" on the reservation without permission from the Sioux.

The Plains tribes would surrender all the rest of their lands to the government. However, as long as there were buffalo to be found, they would be allowed to hunt in "unceded Indian territory," which ran from the Dakota border west to the Bighorn Mountains.

For the next hour the Black Robe spoke of peace, appealing to the Hunkpapas' strong sense of family. "This cruel and unfortunate war must be stopped, not only on account of your children, but for a thousand other reasons." In conclusion, he pleaded, "Forget the past, and accept the offering of peace which is now just sent you."

After Black Moon responded by reciting the Hunkpapas' many complaints against the *Wasichus*, it was Sitting Bull's turn. He had listened carefully to the Black Robe and agreed wholeheartedly with his plea for peace. And he would say as much.

Always a persuasive speaker, Sitting Bull stood up and launched into a long speech. He confessed that during the past four years he had led the Hunkpapas "in bad deeds." He ended by stating that "whatever is done by others, I will submit to, and for all time remain a friend of the whites."

After shaking hands with the Black Robe, who must have been well pleased with the great war chief's friendly words, Sitting Bull sat down. Then, before anyone else could speak, he jumped up. "My friends, I have forgotten two things," he announced, as if he had just remembered them. "I wish all to know that I do not propose to sell any part of my country . . . One thing more: those forts filled with white soldiers must be abandoned; there is no greater source of trouble and grievance to my people."

The next day, Sitting Bull and an *akicita* guard accompanied

59

the Black Robe as far as the Powder River. As an extra precaution, he even assigned eight warriors to escort the priest back to Fort Rice. Although no host could have been warmer or more gracious than Sitting Bull, the message that he sent back with his guest was coldly clear.

He, Sitting Bull, would never touch the pen to the Fort Laramie Treaty, nor would he give up any Hunkpapa land. Furthermore, although the Army may have agreed to abandon the Bozeman Trail forts to the west, the Army forts on the Missouri River were still manned and fortified. Until they, too, were abandoned and Hunkpapa hunting grounds were rid of all *Wasichus*, he would lead the fight against them.

◄ **12** ►

Ye tribes, behold me.
The chiefs of old are gone.
Myself, I shall take courage.

Sitting Bull's
Inauguration Song

When he was a young man, Sitting Bull had been sitting by a lake in the Black Hills when he heard a man's voice singing from a high rock behind him. Telling the story later, Sitting Bull described how he had climbed the rock to find the singer. But when he reached the top, he was surprised to see not a man, but an eagle. As the bird took flight, Sitting Bull realized that through the eagle's song, Wakan Tanka had made him a promise. The old chiefs would go and he would become the leader of all his people.

Years before, a wolf had promised him greatness and he had been elected war chief of the Hunkpapas. Now he had been promised an even higher chieftainship. Sitting Bull remembered the eagle's song and sang it often.

My Father has given me this nation;
In protecting them I have a hard time.

Sitting Bull was already doing everything in his power to protect his people. Determined as ever to drive out the *Wasichus*, he and his war parties terrorized the upper Missouri River countryside. They struck at a fire-boat, military forts, settlers, cattle herders, logging parties, mail carriers, hay cutters, woodchoppers, and any whites who got in their way. They stole horses and mules and killed cattle and oxen.

But the 1868 Fort Laramie Treaty changed everything. Many Sioux chiefs had touched the pen to the treaty, including Gall and the other Hunkpapa warriors who had escorted the Black Robe back to Fort Rice. Tragically, most of them had no understanding of the treaty's complicated terms.

They hadn't understood that they had agreed to live within the boundaries of the Great Sioux Reservation on government agencies. They hadn't understood that they would be permitted to hunt buffalo in the "unceded Indian territory" only until all the buffalo were gone. They also hadn't understood that they were to allow the building of roads and railroads or that they were not to wage war on either the whites or other tribes.

The United States government soon established three Sioux agencies on the Missouri River. Many Sioux families, who had suffered enough from warfare with the Long Knives and their far-shooting guns that killed women and children, "came into" the agencies. As wards of the government, they set up their tipis around the agency buildings, where Indian agents provided them with food and clothing.

Sitting Bull live on an agency and be dependent on *Wasichus* for food and life itself? Never! And he scorned anyone who did.

"The whites may get me at last, as you say, but I will have good times till then," he told a gathering of Hohes. "You are fools to make yourselves slaves to a piece of fat bacon, some hard-tack, and a little sugar and coffee."

Sitting Bull and his uncle Four Horns ignored the treaty. But they weren't able to ignore the reality of hundreds and hundreds of Sioux surrendering to the agencies. At least fewer Hunkpapas went in than any other Sioux tribe.

A wise and farsighted man, Four Horns realized that new times required new remedies. To protect and defend all the people, he envisioned the entire Sioux Nation being united under one supreme war chief.

Although the now-dead Bear's Rib had been appointed chief of the Hunkpapa tribe by General White Beard Harney years ago, a supreme war chief of all seven Sioux tribes was a totally new idea. The Sioux were a warlike people, especially the Hunkpapas. The name Hunkpapa meant "People Who Camp at the Entrance," signifying that the Hunkpapas could be counted on to defend the encampment circle to the death. Because prestige and honor had always been awarded for individual feats of courage, rivalries and jealousies flared up quickly. What man could command such a proud and independent people?

Four Horns knew that the supreme chief couldn't be himself. Even though the bullet that had struck him at Killdeer Mountain had slipped harmlessly into his stomach, or so he said, he was in his fifties and beginning to feel his age. No, the supreme chief should be his nephew Sitting Bull.

Such a momentous step needed approval of the seven Teton

63

Sioux tribes. In 1869, all the tribes except for the Brulés, most of whom had surrendered to the agencies, gathered near Rainy Buttes. Assembling in a great council, the chiefs parleyed. It didn't take them long to agree with Four Horns that a supreme war chief was their one hope for survival. And it didn't take them long to agree that Sitting Bull was the only man who could win loyalty from all the people.

The thousands of Sioux camped at Rainy Buttes voiced their approval. Robert Higheagle explained Sitting Bull's magnetism: "There was something in Sitting Bull that everybody liked. Children liked him because he was kind, the women because he was kind to the family and liked to settle family troubles. Men liked him because he was brave. Medicine men liked him because he was a man they could consider a leader."

Sitting Bull had always believed in Wakan Tanka's promise of leadership, but now that it had come to pass, he felt humbled. No Sioux warrior had ever been elevated so high. He would be responsible for protecting not only his Icira band and his Hunkpapa tribe, but also the whole Sioux Nation. He knew that he could do it. He had to do it. With the people putting their lives in his trust, he had no other choice. And he considered himself fortunate that his daring Oglala warrior-friend Crazy Horse would be his second in command.

Rainy Buttes came through with a beautiful clear day for the inauguration. As Sitting Bull waited in his tipi for the ceremony to begin, he must have experienced a range of emotions: pride, joy, excitement, fulfillment, and maybe even nervousness about the ceremony to come. Four thousand Sioux and even some Cheyennes would be witness to his inauguration.

And then there wasn't any more time for reflection. Four

Horns and three other chiefs arrived. They led Sitting Bull out of his tipi and seated him on a buffalo robe. With the four chiefs holding the four corners of the robe, he was carried to the council lodge, four being a sacred and lucky number.

The ceremony began with the lighting of the sacred pipe, as did every Sioux ceremony and council. It was only after the mystical White Buffalo Maiden had presented the Sacred Calf Pipe to the Sioux many generations before that they had come together as a people. It was also when they had entered into communion with Wakan Tanka, as well as the earth, four winds, and all the natural universe. The Sacred Calf Pipe became a symbol of peace with family and friends, and smoking the pipe together created a bond of good faith.

Lame Deer expressed what smoking the sacred pipe meant to him: "I knew that within this pipe was me. I knew that when I smoked it I was at the center of things, giving myself to the Great Spirit, and that every other Indian praying with this pipe would, at one time or the other, feel the same."

On this occasion, Sitting Bull was given the sacred pipe to be treasured always. He received other gifts, too: a bow and ten arrows, a flintlock gun, and a magnificent warbonnet with a long double tail that swept the ground. The bonnet held special significance for Sitting Bull, as well it might have. Each of its three hundred eagle feathers had been given by a warrior to represent one of his brave deeds.

The rest of the day was filled with festivities, dancing, singing, and speeches. As master of ceremonies, Four Horns spoke to Sitting Bull, not as an uncle speaking to his nephew, but as a lesser chief speaking to his superior.

"For your bravery on the battlefields and as the greatest warrior of our Bands, we have elected you our War Chief the leader of the entire Sioux nation!" he proclaimed. "When you tell us to fight, we shall fight, when you tell us to make peace, we shall make peace."

At the end of the celebration, Gall and Running Antelope lifted Sitting Bull onto a handsome bay horse. Members of the *akicita* societies mounted and lined up behind him, their faces and horses painted and their sacred shields uncovered. Bright pennants fluttered from every lance as Sitting Bull led the procession slowly around the camp circles to the sound of four thousand voices raised in song.

Looking into the expectant faces of his people, Sitting Bull must have been deeply affected, for his voice rang out above the others:

> *"Ye tribes, behold me.*
> *The chiefs of old are gone.*
> *Myself, I shall take courage."*

‹ 13 ›

The Crow Indians I look for them
I found them
So their horses I brought home.

Hunkpapa War Song

Sitting Bull and his Hunkpapas fought the Crows in one battle after another during the late 1860s. Much as they may have wanted to rid the plains of the hated Long Knives, their very survival depended on taking over the Crows' hunting grounds.

The buffalo herds were disappearing from their usual range and roaming into Crow territory to the west. As the lifeblood of the Sioux, buffalo provided them with food, shelter, clothing, bedding, fuel, weapons, tools, utensils, containers, thread, glue, and much, much more. And so the Hunkpapas, along with their Oglala, Miniconjou, Sans Arc, Two Kettles, and Blackfeet-Sioux cousins, followed the buffalo west, fighting the Crows the whole way.

Even the oldest ones alive couldn't remember a time when

the Sioux and the Crows hadn't been at war. Certainly every Hunkpapa knew that one Hunkpapa fighting man was worth three cowardly Crows. On the other hand, the Crows laughed at the Hunkpapa warriors, calling them "women" because they parted their hair in the middle, just like the Crow women.

The two tribes may have called each other cowardly, but in the winter of 1869 they fought a savage battle in which there were no cowards. Sitting Bull and his Hunkpapas were camped along the edge of Crow country on the upper Missouri River. It was during the wood-cracking moon, the coldest time of the winter.

Two Hunkpapa boys who were out hunting were attacked by a party of thirty Crows on foot. The Crows killed one boy and wounded the other. When the wounded boy finally made it back to camp and told everyone what had happened, Sitting Bull erupted in fury. Thirty Crows attacking two young boys? Those Crows had to be taught a lesson.

"*Hopo! Hopo!* Let's go! Let's go! Take action!" he shouted to his warriors.

Eager for revenge, one hundred men joined Sitting Bull's war party, including Jumping Bull, Four Horns, and Sitting Bull's youngest uncle, Looks-for-Him. Sitting Bull, who wore robes with hair on the inside and calf-high moccasins lined with buffalo wool, had his party start off at night despite the frigid winter weather. Although the war party followed the Crows' tracks easily enough through the snow, the Crows had anticipated their coming and taken refuge behind a rocky fortification at the head of Big Dry Creek.

The Hunkpapas attacked at dawn. But the Crows were pretty

much invincible behind their rocky breastworks. Every time the Hunkpapas charged, a relentless barrage of Crow bullets and arrows forced them to retreat. As fronter, Sitting Bull led his men in daring. He dashed in, got off a few shots, and then pulled back when the firing got too heavy.

About noon Sitting Bull lost patience and called to his warriors that he would mount the barricade. "We must not let them escape. I'll go first, you follow," he ordered.

But Jumping Bull stepped forward with an offer. "I will first empty their guns," he proposed.

Riding close to the Crows, Jumping Bull circled again and again as the Crows kept up a steady firing. Just as Jumping Bull had anticipated, they used up much of their ammunition without hitting him.

Now it was time to take the offensive. With his war party behind him, Sitting Bull dismounted and ran toward the Crows as fast as his limp would allow. Scaling the rocks to the top, he and his Hunkpapas dropped down on the other side. In vicious hand-to-hand fighting, they killed every last Crow.

Although it was a triumphant victory, the Hunkpapas paid a steep penalty: thirteen warriors dead and seventeen wounded. Sitting Bull was among the mourners. He returned to camp with the body of his uncle Looks-for-Him, who had been shot through the breast. Grieving, Sitting Bull cut his hair, covered himself with mud, and went without leggings or moccasins despite the deep snow and freezing temperatures. To commemorate one of the most ferocious battles they ever fought against the Crows, the Hunkpapas named the year 1869 "When-Thirty-Crows-Were-Killed" in their picture calendar.

The following summer the Hunkpapas were camped in a large village of Oglalas, Miniconjous, and Sans Arcs on the Yellowstone River, below the mouth of the Rosebud. One day, Sitting Bull withdrew from the others and walked away, singing. When he returned, he announced that a vision had come to him. He had seen himself fighting against tribal enemies in two days' time.

"Many enemies and several Sioux will be killed," he said, adding, "I saw a ball of fire—a spark—coming toward me. But it disappeared when it reached me."

No one had to interpret Sitting Bull's vision. Everyone who heard it knew that he would be wounded in the fight to come. And so did he.

Now that Sitting Bull was thirty-nine, his mother, Her-Holy-Door, may have understandably tried to talk him out of going. But Sitting Bull was supreme war chief, and a determined one at that. Neither his mother nor the threat of being wounded could stop him.

The next day he rode out at the head of four hundred warriors. Receiving news from scouts that a Flathead camp was on the Musselshell River, the war party traveled all night. Sitting Bull had already mapped out their strategy.

An advance party of some forty men rode into the Flathead camp and stole a few horses. When a hundred Flatheads mounted and took off after them, the advance party headed for the main body of Sioux warriors, who were lying in ambush. It was the old decoy trick, but it worked.

The war party swarmed out of hiding, and a hot fight followed. Although a number of Sioux warriors were wounded, the Flatheads were outnumbered four to one, and before long they withdrew. Rather than pursuing them, the Miniconjou chief Flying-By called a halt to the fighting.

"Stop! That will be all for this time! Some good men have been wounded already," he cried.

Although most of the Sioux turned back for home, Sitting Bull refused to let the Flatheads get away so easily. Six other warriors chose to stay behind, too. Soon a number of Flatheads returned to retrieve their dead, just as Sitting Bull had anticipated. With a whoop and a war cry, he charged the Flathead party, with his six comrades close behind him. The Flatheads headed for their village at a gallop, all but one who dismounted. As Sitting Bull rode in to steal his horse, the Flathead raised his rifle and fired. The bullet struck Sitting Bull's left arm, burning like fire.

The fight with the Flatheads didn't accomplish much except to raise Sitting Bull even higher in the eyes of his people. Not only had his vision of a battle in two days' time come to pass, but he had gone willingly into the fight, knowing that he would be wounded. Even though his wound healed quickly, Her-Holy-Door was perhaps the only one to despair of her stubborn son.

Over the next few years, Sitting Bull and his Hunkpapa warriors continued to wage war on the Crows. With each victory, they acquired more and more of the Crows' hunting grounds. But the victories went both ways.

In 1871 a Crow war party crept into the Hunkpapas' camp at night and stole their pony herd as the Hunkpapas slept. As far as White Bull was concerned, that was the way the Crows always fought. "They never attack by day but sneak around at night like coyotes," he jeered. Nevertheless, the theft was enough of an event for the Hunkpapas to call the year 1871 in their picture calendar "Chasing-Horses-in-Camp."

During another battle with the Crows, Sitting Bull noticed that a young Crow warrior had used up all of his arrows. Shooting two arrows over to the Crow, Sitting Bull waited while his foe placed one of the arrows in his bowstring. Without pausing to give Sitting Bull a chance, the Crow shot the arrow. It glanced off Sitting Bull's wrist. Luckily, the wound was so slight that it didn't stop Sitting Bull from taking aim and shooting the Crow through the stomach, killing him instantly. It can be imagined what Her-Holy-Door had to say when her son returned with yet another wound.

An old-timer sympathized. "Sitting Bull surely had the endurance of a buffalo bull experiencing all kinds of hardships on the war-path," he remarked.

Before long, the Hunkpapas and their Sioux allies had pushed the Crows all the way back to the Bighorn Mountains. The Sioux now reigned over the whole Yellowstone River valley, which was rich in game beyond imagining, with herds of buffalo and bands of elk, antelope, black-tailed deer, and bighorn sheep. The rivers abounded with beaver, muskrat, otter, ducks, geese, swans, and all kinds of fish.

Sitting Bull knew that this vast Yellowstone country was where he and his people were destined to raise their children. And he would defend to the death their right to stay, whether it meant fighting the Crows, the Flatheads . . . or the Long Knives.

‹ **14** ›

We are the pride of the Army,
And a regiment of great renown,
Our name's on the pages of history
From sixty-six on down.
If you think we stop or falter
While into the fray we're goin',
Just watch the step, with our heads erect
When our band plays "Garry Owen."

Custer's Seventh Cavalry Marching Song

Sitting Bull and his people couldn't ask for anything more than to live and hunt in the magnificent Yellowstone River country. But the *Wasichus* had plans for the Yellowstone country, too. Big plans. In the fall of 1871, surveyors, escorted by six hundred infantrymen, appeared in the Yellowstone valley to survey for a railroad.

"Be a little against fighting but when anyone shoots be ready to fight," Four Horns had advised Sitting Bull at the time of his inauguration as supreme war chief.

Sitting Bull had listened, considered his uncle's advice, and decided to follow it. He and Crazy Horse had agreed that they would fight the Long Knives only if the Long Knives attacked first or if the Long Knives invaded Sioux hunting grounds.

For the time being, the two leaders kept to their peace pact and took no action against the surveyors. However, Sitting Bull wasn't going to let the incident go unnoticed. In November 1871 he sent Black Moon to meet with government officials at the Fort Peck trading post. During the council, Black Moon protested that the Yellowstone country was Sioux country and the Sioux would never allow a railroad to cross it.

Having been generous once, Sitting Bull and Crazy Horse weren't so open-minded the following summer. In August 1872 they were leading a war party of some one thousand Hunkpapas, Oglalas, Miniconjous, Sans Arcs, and Blackfeet-Sioux against the Crows when scouts reported in. Another survey party had invaded the Yellowstone country. Accompanied by five hundred Long Knives, the surveyors were camped on the north side of the Yellowstone River, opposite Arrow Creek.

Sitting Bull knew that this time they would have to do something, and he called all the chiefs together. As they met in council, the young warriors took matters into their own hands. As ambitious to win war honors as Sitting Bull had been at their age, they crept past the *akicita* guard that had been posted. Sneaking into the Long Knives' camp, they stole Army horses and personal belongings. By daybreak, serious fighting had broken out.

Before long, the young warriors were riding back and forth on the daring line within shooting distance of the Long Knives. Sitting Bull and Crazy Horse, who were overseeing the battle from a bluff, may have been friends, but they were also proud warriors. Crazy Horse made the first move. He rode down from the bluff and out onto the daring line. Slowly he walked his horse along the line. Army bullets flew all around him as his Oglala comrades shouted out his name and cheered his bravery.

As supreme war chief, Sitting Bull wasn't about to allow Crazy Horse to best him. Dressed only in a plain shirt and leggings, he walked down from the bluff, made his way onto the daring line with his usual short-step gait, and sat down. Bullets whined overhead and pocked the ground around him as he took out his long-stemmed pipe from its pouch, filled and lit it. Pointing first to the sky, the earth, and the four directions, he then began to smoke.

"Any Indians who wish to smoke with me, come on!" he called.

Taking up the challenge, his nephew White Bull and three others ran out to join him. Sitting Bull passed the pipe from one to another.

"Our hearts beat rapidly, and we smoked as fast as we could," White Bull recalled. "All around us the bullets were kicking up the dust. But Sitting Bull was not afraid."

After he had smoked the pipe down, Sitting Bull cleaned the bowl and replaced the pipe in its pouch. As the guns continued to blaze, he limped back to his own lines while the other four raced on ahead.

Crazy Horse again rode along the daring line, but Sitting Bull's brave deed clearly won the war honors of the day and everyone knew it. Acts of courage, however, couldn't overcome the Long Knives' firepower, and in the end, Sitting Bull and his war party were driven back.

Only a week later, they confronted the Long Knives again. Still determined to oust these intruders, Sitting Bull headed an attack on a military expedition at O'Fallon Creek. With Sitting Bull directing the action, some of the war party pressed from the rear, while others stationed themselves on nearby bluffs and fired down on the Army's wagon trains. Although they harassed the troops almost all the way back to Fort Rice, they didn't do much damage. At least Sitting Bull had the satisfaction of shouting at the troops that if the railroad went through, he would summon all the tribes and wipe out every last soldier and worker.

Apparently the *Wasichus* weren't worried. The following summer, 1873, the railroad surveyors returned again. This time their escort included the Seventh Cavalry, commanded by Lieutenant Colonel George A. Custer. Known as Long Hair because of his shoulder-length red-gold hair, Custer was no stranger to the Great Plains. Five years before, he and his Seventh Cavalry had attacked a sleeping Cheyenne village on the Washita River and killed more than a hundred men, women, and children. Afterward, a number of the Cheyenne survivors had ridden north and joined Sitting Bull's camp.

It wasn't until August 1873 that Sitting Bull and some four hundred lodges of Hunkpapas, Miniconjous, and Cheyennes realized that the *Wasichus* were back. Not only were they back, but the Sioux encampment on the Yellowstone River was directly in their line of march. Quickly Sitting Bull and Crazy Horse made plans to trap the Long Knives in an ambush.

But when the Cheyenne warriors who had survived the Washita massacre heard the familiar Seventh Cavalry "Garry Owen" marching music, they broke out of hiding. In a frenzy to get at Long Hair and his men, they charged, war whooping and shrieking. At the break in ranks, the other warriors charged too.

Long Hair Custer and his troops were able to defend themselves until reinforcements arrived and routed the war party. As always, the safety of the women and children was on everybody's mind. Riding hard back to camp, the chiefs ordered the women to pack up their tipis and belongings. With the Long Knives in pursuit, the chiefs had all the people cross the Yellowstone River to the south bank. They paddled across in bull boats, circular tubs covered with buffalo hides. Although the Sioux' sturdy little horses easily swam across the rapid, deep river, the Long Knives' big American horses couldn't make it.

The next day, Sitting Bull called out encouragement to his men from a high bluff on the south side of the Yellowstone. While warriors kept up a steady firing at the Long Knives, who had spent the night on the north bank, Crazy Horse led a war party across the river. Some of the war party landed above the Long Knives and some landed below. Once again the strains of "Garry Owen" echoed across the river to where Sitting Bull was overseeing the battle. And once again the Army's heavy weaponry drove the warriors back.

With both sides claiming a victory, the two forces went their separate ways. The Long Knives under Custer marched back to Fort Abraham Lincoln, another new Army fort on the Missouri River. Sitting Bull, Crazy Horse, and their people headed up the Bighorn River to spend the rest of the summer hunting buffalo and fighting Crows. Plans for the railroad were abandoned. Although Sitting Bull no doubt believed that he and his war parties had driven off the *Wasichus,* the reality was that the project had run out of money.

Despite having reached his forties, Sitting Bull had plunged wholeheartedly into the fighting. Even more important, he had directed the battles and emboldened his warriors and their Cheyenne allies by singing brave-heart songs and encouraging his men.

A Cheyenne warrior described Sitting Bull's well-earned fame: "There was only one who was considered as being above all others. This was Sitting Bull."

The people of America were beginning to take notice of Sitting Bull, too. In 1865 his name had been mentioned for the first time in an official Army report. As the years went by, he had been increasingly written and talked about. When the battles of Arrow Creek, O'Fallon Creek, and the Yellowstone were reported in eastern newspapers and journals, Sitting Bull was thundered against as a blackhearted villain. Some even called the violence that had begun to rock the northern Great Plains "Sitting Bull's War." Perhaps it was an appropriate title.

‹ 15 ›

Friends, what are you talking about?
The Black Hills belong to me
Saying this I took fresh courage.

Sitting Bull's Song

Rumors of gold in the Black Hills had been circulating around the United States for years. The Black Hills, however, were within the Great Sioux Reservation, and the 1868 Fort Laramie Treaty banned whites from entering any part of the reservation without permission.

Ban or no ban, in the summer of 1874, Long Hair Custer led more than a thousand men into the Black Hills to the strains of his favorite marching tune, "Garry Owen." Although they were supposedly surveying for a fort, they were on a quest for gold. A fort or gold didn't matter to the Sioux. They called Custer's trail the Thieves' Road and Custer Chief of the Thieves. And thieves they were. They found gold, and lots of it. As soon as word got out, there was no stopping the stampede into the Black Hills.

Because the Black Hills' dark ponderosa pines appeared black from a distance, the Sioux also called the hills Paha Sapa, or "hills that are black." Their pine forests, majestic mountain peaks, and clear-running streams contrasted sharply with the surrounding treeless plains. When food was scarce, the Sioux wintered or hunted there, but basically Paha Sapa was held in sacred trust for Wakan Tanka and religious ceremonies. "The land known as the Black Hills is considered by the Indians to be the center of their land," a Hunkpapa war chief declared.

Although Sitting Bull was far to the north fighting the Crows, word soon reached him of Long Hair's invasion of Paha Sapa. The Sioux had been lied to again. Special and sacred, Paha Sapa was forbidden to all *Wasichus,* especially the hated Long Knives.

Sitting Bull was now a high-ranking member of the elite Silent Eater Society. Unlike the *akicita* societies, the Silent Eaters didn't sing, dance, boast, or tell jokes. They met secretly at night to eat and discuss how they could best serve their people. Now, speaking as an influential leader of the Silent Eaters and supreme war chief, Sitting Bull proposed a united front. This newest outrage was a matter for the Cheyennes, too, not just the Sioux.

In the summer of 1875, Sitting Bull brought the Hunkpapas and the Northern Cheyennes together in a ceremonial Sun Dance to seal the bonds of friendship between them. Dressed in a breechcloth, moccasins, and warbonnet, with his body painted yellow, Sitting Bull rode to the Sun Dance circle on a handsome black horse that the Cheyenne holy man Ice had given him.

"I wish my friends to fill one pipe and I wish my people to fill one pipe," he ordered.

Under Sitting Bull's direction, the Hunkpapas and the Cheyennes symbolically smoked each other's pipes and sang and danced together as one. And as one they looked up to Sitting Bull.

"He had come into admiration by all Indians as a man whose medicine was good," the Cheyenne warrior Wooden Leg said, "that is, as a man having a kind heart and good judgment as to the best course of conduct. He was considered as being altogether brave, but peaceable."

Much as Sitting Bull may have wanted peace, peace wasn't always possible. Because the Army made only feeble attempts to keep out the miners, nearly fifteen thousand gold rushers had overrun the Black Hills by the summer of 1875. Americans everywhere were encouraging their government to take over the hills from those other Americans whom they called "savages."

The government didn't need much encouragement. A commission was sent from Washington to the Red Cloud Agency in September 1875. Its members were prepared to offer the Sioux six million dollars for the Black Hills, or four hundred thousand dollars a year for rights to mine its gold. Terms of the Fort Laramie Treaty had stated that "at least three-fourths of all the adult male Indians" had to sign their approval before any land in the Great Sioux Reservation could change hands. To get the needed number of signatures, the commission dispatched runners into the countryside to invite the northern hunting bands to come in.

To Sitting Bull's astonishment one of the runners who arrived at his camp was his adopted brother Frank Grouard, the Grabber. Two years before, the two men had argued when the Grabber had lied to Sitting Bull about a trip that he had made to the Fort Peck trading post. Escaping Sitting Bull's wrath, the Grabber had left the Hunkpapas to live with Crazy Horse and his Oglalas.

Meeting with Sitting Bull was a waste of the Grabber's time anyway. In a long speech, Sitting Bull made it clear that he would never agree to selling Paha Sapa, nor would he ever come in. He was no "coffee cooler" Indian and never would be.

The commission's meeting at the Red Cloud Agency was a waste of time too. Even though ten thousand Indians attended, most of whom already lived on agencies, Crazy Horse's warriors broke up the council in a dramatic armed charge. Sitting Bull was well satisfied when he heard the news.

"These hills are a treasure to us Indians," he said. "That is the food pack of the people and when the poor have nothing to eat we can all go there and have something to eat."

Despite their failure, government officials were far from admitting defeat. If they couldn't buy the Black Hills, then they would take them by force. After all, went their excuse, the Sioux were still fighting the Crows in violation of the Fort Laramie Treaty. Furthermore, the Sioux and the Northern Cheyennes were terrorizing the whites in the northern Dakota and Montana territories in another violation of the treaty. "Sitting Bull and his band of murdering robbers" was how the governor of the Montana Territory described Sitting Bull and his warriors.

"Murdering robbers" wasn't quite the term Sitting Bull

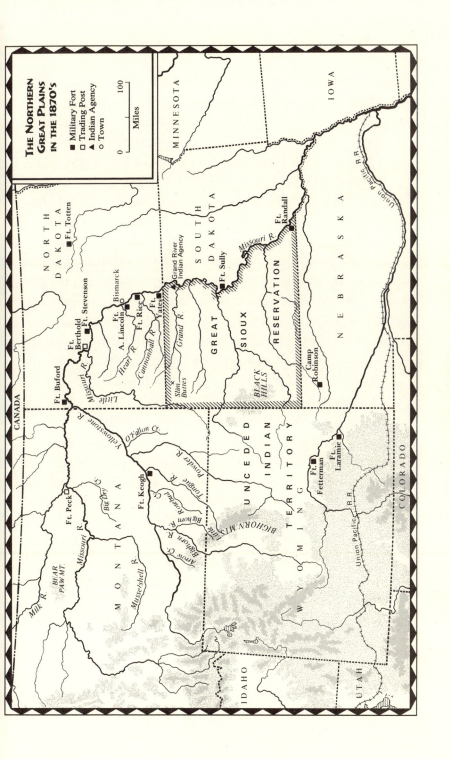

THE NORTHERN
GREAT PLAINS
IN THE 1870'S

■ Military Fort
□ Trading Post
▲ Indian Agency
○ Town

0   100
Miles

CANADA

MONTANA

Milk R.

BEAR PAW MT.

Missouri R.

Musselshell R.

Big Dry Cr.

Yellowstone R.

O'Fallon Cr.

Ft. Peck

Ft. Keogh

Powder R.

Tongue R.

Rosebud Cr.

Big horn R.

Little Bighorn R.

Arrow Cr.

BIGHORN MTS.

IDAHO

UTAH

WYOMING

Union Pacific R.R.

COLORADO

UNCEDED INDIAN TERRITORY

Ft. Fetterman

Ft. Laramie

NORTH DAKOTA

Ft. Totten

Ft. Buford

Ft. Berthold

Ft. Stevenson

Bismarck

A. Lincoln

Ft. Rice

Ft. Yates

Grand River Indian Agency

Heart R.

Cannonball R.

Grand R.

Little Missouri R.

Missouri R.

Slim Butes

SOUTH DAKOTA

Ft. Sully

Missouri R.

Ft. Randall

GREAT SIOUX RESERVATION

BLACK HILLS

Camp Robinson

NEBRASKA

Union Pacific RR

MINNESOTA

IOWA

would have used. Of course he and his warriors fought the Crows. They always had and they always would. And if any settlers, trappers, or miners were trespassing on "unceded Indian territory," where they had no right to be, then they had only themselves to blame for what happened to them.

Apparently neither the president nor Congress was concerned that its own citizens were also violating the Fort Laramie Treaty. All they cared about was acquiring the gold-rich Black Hills. To make their seizure of the land appear legal, runners were once more sent out to all the northern hunting camps in December 1875. This time they brought an order for all the people to surrender to an agency on the Great Sioux Reservation by January 31, 1876. If they didn't surrender, armed troops would bring them in. With all the Indians settled on agencies, the government could then simply take over the "unceded Indian territory" as well as the Black Hills.

When the runners arrived at Sitting Bull's camp on the Yellowstone River after braving blizzards and bitter cold, neither Sitting Bull nor anyone else understood that the order amounted to a declaration of war. They considered it to be just another summons to yet another council. Furthermore, the deadline of January 31 meant nothing to a people who had no knowledge of the *Wasichu* calendar. Who would travel all that distance in the middle of a Plains winter anyway? Cordial as always, Sitting Bull sent his reply back with the runners. Maybe he would come in later to trade, like next summer.

There was nothing cordial about the government's reaction when the deadline passed with no hunting bands surrendering. Convinced that all it would take to acquire the Black Hills and the "unceded Indian territory" was a few skirmishes, the War Department ordered the troops out.

War it would be.

◂ 16 ▸

*Friends, whatever you council about
I consider a difficult undertaking.*

Hunkpapa Council Song

On a bitterly cold March 17, 1876, Colonel J. J. Reynolds and his troops attacked a sleeping village on the Powder River. Seven hundred Oglalas and Cheyennes were on their way in to surrender at an agency. Awakened by the cavalry's gunfire, men, women, and children rushed out of their tipis only to be met by the Long Knives riding through their camp, shooting at anything that moved.

The Cheyenne Wooden Leg described the horror: "Women screamed. Children cried for their mothers. Old people tottered and hobbled away to get out of reach of the bullets singing among the lodges."

The warriors took cover where they could find it, firing back to give their women and children time to retreat to the high rock bluffs behind camp. As soon as they saw that their families were safe, they headed for the bluffs too. From their protected position, they kept up a steady barrage of gunfire. Unable to get at the armed warriors, the troops finally gave up and withdrew about two o'clock in the afternoon. As a parting gesture, they stole half of the camp's herd of fourteen hundred horses and mules and then set fire to all the tipis and everything in them: stored food, supplies, and clothing. The next day the warriors trailed the Long Knives, sneaked into their camp, and recaptured all of their animals.

Any thought that the Oglalas and Cheyennes might have had of surrendering vanished with the first gunshot. Instead, they turned around and headed back to Crazy Horse's camp. With little clothing and no food, they struggled through the snow in temperatures that hovered around forty degrees below zero. But Crazy Horse and his people didn't have enough food and shelter for so many. Packing up their camp, they escorted the frozen survivors to Sitting Bull's camp farther down the Powder River.

Sitting Bull's Hunkpapas were as generous as he was. A grateful Cheyenne remembered their warm welcome: "Uncpapa (Hunkpapa) women had set their pots to boiling when first we had been seen. Now they came with meat. They kept coming, coming, with more and more meat . . . Women and girls came with gifts."

The raid on the sleeping village was imaginatively called the Battle of Powder River by the Army. Whatever it was called, when the Oglalas and Cheyennes told Sitting Bull about the attack, he was enraged. By putting women and children at risk, the Long Knives had struck at the very heart of Sioux life. And Sitting Bull had double reason for his fury. The only white person who could have followed the trail to the village at night was the Grabber.

Sitting Bull had saved the Grabber's life, called him Brother, welcomed him into his family tipi, and taught him the ways of the Sioux. He had to admit it, Gall and No Neck had been right and he had been wrong.

"One time that man should have been killed and I kept him and now he has joined the soldiers," Sitting Bull stormed. "He was no good and should be killed."

But Sitting Bull had more important matters on his mind than revenge on the Grabber. Although he and Crazy Horse had kept to their peace pact, the Long Knives had now made it clear that they were prepared to steal Paha Sapa over the bodies of women and children. Their savage attack called for strong measures.

As supreme war chief, Sitting Bull put out a call to all the hunting bands to assemble. The Oglalas, Sans Arcs, Miniconjous, as well as some Brulés, Blackfeet-Sioux, Two Kettles, Yanktonai, Dakotas, Northern Cheyennes, and the Sioux' new allies, the Northern Arapahoes, rode in from every direction.

Sitting Bull, who was wise in the ways of head warriors, summoned the chiefs to a great council. A powerful speaker, he was at his most effective as he addressed the distinguished gathering.

"We are an island of Indians in a lake of whites," he asserted. "We must stand together, or they will rub us out separately.

These soldiers have come shooting; they want war. All right, we'll give it to them!"

The chiefs shouted their approval.

War it would be.

‹ 17 ›

You tribes, what are you saying?
I have been a war chief.
All the same, I'm still living.

Sitting Bull's Song

As soon as the ice on the rivers broke up in the spring of 1876 and the grass grew lush and green, Sitting Bull sent out runners to the agencies with a message: "Come to my camp at the Big Bend of the Rosebud. Let's all get together and have one big fight with the soldiers!"

Ever since the Fort Laramie Treaty had been signed in 1868, more and more Sioux had surrendered to the government agencies. By 1876 there were some ten thousand Sioux living on agencies, with only about three thousand Sioux still out. A number of those agency people spent the warmer months in the northern camps, hunting, visiting relatives, and fighting. Others never left the agencies at all. Now Sitting Bull's call tempted many agency families to slip away and head north where the hunting bands had already gathered.

There was nothing that the Sioux liked better than a get-to-gether, and what a get-together this one turned out to be. There was feasting, singing, dancing, boys racing their ponies, young couples courting, women renewing friendships, and old men reliving ancient battles. To find enough game and fire-wood, as well as grass for their huge pony herds, the camp had to move every few days.

The Northern Cheyennes led the line of march that extended for miles, while the Hunkpapas brought up the rear. The Chey-enne Wooden Leg made it clear why these two positions were the most respected . . . and dangerous: "The Cheyennes kept scouts out in front looking forward from high points. The Unc-papas (Hunkpapas) had always some of their young men stay-ing back to observe if any enemies were following."

Sitting Bull seemed to be everywhere at once in that vast camp. He held councils with Crazy Horse and the other chiefs. He advised the camp criers what announcements they should herald. He sent out the young warriors to steal horses and guns, especially guns. A young warrior remembered Sitting Bull during that time: "In those days only one thing smelled good to him—gunpowder."

But Sitting Bull had always been, and always would be, more than a war chief, and he kept everyone's spirits up with both speeches and song. Riding through camp, he would en-courage his people by singing:

> *"You tribes, what are you saying?*
> *I have been a war chief.*
> *All the same, I'm still living."*

91

Of all his roles, perhaps the one that mattered most to both him and his people was that of holy man. In late May 1876 he climbed a high butte to be alone to pray. Falling asleep, he had a dream in which he saw a dark cloud of mounted soldiers roar in from the east and overtake a white cloud, which represented his people's encampment. Thunder boomed, lightning flashed, and a drenching rain fell. When the storm was over, the dark cloud had vanished and the white cloud was drifting peacefully out of sight. Calling his chiefs together, Sitting Bull interpreted his vision. Although mounted soldiers would attack their village, the Sioux would defeat them. He added a warning. Scouts must keep a sharp watch out for Long Knives marching from the east.

A week later Sitting Bull asked White Bull, Jumping Bull, and Black Moon's son to accompany him to a hilltop. Wearing plain dress, with no paint or feathers, Sitting Bull had his companions join him in a pipe ceremony after which he prayed. Facing the sun, he promised to perform a Sun Dance, as well as kill a buffalo as an offering to Wakan Tanka.

Immediately afterward, Sitting Bull went hunting and killed three buffalo. Selecting the best one, a fat cow, he stretched it out on the ground, raised his hands high, and presented it to Wakan Tanka.

The Sun Dance was held two days later, with Sitting Bull as Leader and Black Moon as Intercessor. Although Sitting Bull's back and chest were already scarred from earlier Sun Dances, in this Sun Dance he was going to offer his flesh. A fellow warrior explained: "A man's body is his own, and when he gives his body or his flesh he is giving the only thing which really belongs to him."

Sensing the significance of Sitting Bull's sacrifice, hundreds of onlookers crowded around the Sun Dance circle. After he had completed his sweat bath and had smoked, sung, and danced, Sitting Bull sat with his back against the sacred pole and his legs outstretched. Jumping Bull knelt beside him. Starting with Sitting Bull's left arm, near the wrist, Jumping Bull lifted a small piece of skin with a sharp awl and then cut the flesh with a knife. He held the piece of flesh to the sky and announced, "This man promised to give you his flesh; he now fulfills his vow."

Working as quickly as he could, Jumping Bull sliced fifty pieces of flesh from each of his adopted brother's arms. The ceremony took about half an hour, with Sitting Bull wailing the whole time, not because of the agonizing pain, but to plead with Wakan Tanka to be merciful to his people.

When Jumping Bull was finished, Sitting Bull stood, faced the sun, and began to dance. He danced all that day and night and into the second day. About noon, the spectators noticed that he seemed to be in a faint, although he didn't fall. Black Moon eased him to the ground and revived him with water. Raising his head, Sitting Bull whispered to Black Moon, who in turn repeated his words to the hushed gathering. When Sitting Bull had looked up, he had seen soldiers and horses falling like grasshoppers from the sky. Their heads were down and their hats were tumbling off as they fell upside down into the Sioux camp.

"I give you these because they have no ears," a voice had said.

What a glorious vision! Sitting Bull had foreseen that the Long Knives would fall into camp, attack the Sioux, and all be killed. But Sitting Bull had a warning. The people must not steal anything from the bodies, not guns, horses, clothing, or possessions.

"Kill them but don't take anything," he cautioned. "If you take spoils you will starve at the white man's door."

The elated people weren't listening. All they heard was that Sitting Bull had twice envisioned their victory over the Long Knives and that was all they cared about.

◂ 18 ▸

Friends, try our Best
I don't want my father to be made ashamed
Because he is Chief.

White Bull's Song After
the Battle of the Rosebud

A week after what became known as Sitting Bull's Sun Dance, scouts posted on a hilltop overlooking the Sioux and Cheyenne encampment sounded an alarm.

"Waoo-oo-oo-oo!" they wolf-howled.

They had seen soldiers, many soldiers, on the march along the Rosebud valley. General George Crook, known as Three Stars, was at the head of more than a thousand soldiers and almost three hundred Crow and Shoshone scouts.

Mount up! Prepare for war! was the hot-blooded young warriors' immediate response. In his youth Sitting Bull might have responded the same way, but now that he was supreme war chief, his people depended on him. After meeting with Crazy Horse and the other headmen, he sent criers through the camps with an order: "Young men, leave the soldiers alone unless they attack us."

Despite the order, a fight beckoned and the young men couldn't resist. Wooden Leg was as fired up as the others. "Warriors came from every camp circle. We had our weapons, war clothing, paints and medicine. I had my six-shooter," he recalled.

That night five hundred ambitious young men stole out of camp and headed for the Rosebud. When Sitting Bull and Crazy Horse heard about their stunt, they realized that there was no holding back the rest of the young warriors either, and they agreed to lead the war party. But Sitting Bull's visions had predicted that soldiers would attack their camp. Half of the warriors must stay behind to guard the women and children.

When the war party prepared to leave the next morning, Sitting Bull was still so weak from his Sun Dance and his arms were so painfully swollen that he had to be helped onto his horse. Knowing that he wouldn't be able to fight, he wore ordinary dress, with two feathers in his hair.

As dawn broke, Sitting Bull and Crazy Horse rode out of camp and headed for Rosebud Creek, some forty miles away. Rosebud Creek flowed through the middle of a mile-wide valley broken up by rocks, scrubby trees, and shrubs. Sitting Bull knew the territory well. It was where he and his Hunkpapas had skirmished with the Canadian Métis just three years before. Because the Métis had fought from behind defensive earthen barricades, the Hunkpapas had named the year 1873 "Fighting-in-Trenches."

As they approached the familiar valley at the head of eight hundred warriors on June 17, 1876, Sitting Bull and Crazy Horse hoped to launch a surprise attack. But Crow and Shoshone scouts spotted them. While some of the enemy scouts raced back to alert Three Stars, the rest kept the Sioux and Cheyennes at bay until the troops arrived. By nine o'clock in the morning, the battle was raging.

Although he was barely able to sit his horse, Sitting Bull emboldened his warriors. "Be of steady mind—remember how to hold a gun and shoot them," he called. "Brace up, now! Brace up!"

Whether or not it was Sitting Bull's rallying cries that inspired his warriors, they fought with a new determination and skill. Instead of riding in, counting coup, getting off a few shots, and then circling back to their own lines, they fought together as a unified war party, attacking fiercely again and again.

Wooden Leg described the day-long battle: "Until the sun went far toward the west there were charges back and forth. Our Indians fought and ran away, fought and ran away. The soldiers and their Indian scouts did the same. Sometimes we chased them, sometimes they chased us."

During the fight, a Cheyenne war chief's horse was shot out from under him. Seemingly out of nowhere, the chief's sister, Buffalo Calf Road Woman, who had accompanied the war party, charged into the fray on her mount. She swung her brother up behind her and rode him to safety.

By late afternoon Three Stars Crook admitted defeat. Stunned by the warriors' new tactics, he pulled his men out of the Battle of the Rosebud and headed south. Standing Bear told how he watched them go: "When we got on top of the ridge we could see the soldiers of Three Stars retreating toward

Goose Creek a long way off. A big dust was rising there. Then we went home."

The Sioux named the battle "The Fight with Three Stars." In honor of Buffalo Calf Road Woman's daring rescue, the Cheyennes called it "Where the Girl Saved Her Brother." Although his war party had clearly been victorious, Sitting Bull knew that it wasn't the victory that he had envisioned. The soldiers hadn't attacked the Sioux encampment and they hadn't all been killed. That victory was still to come.

◄ **19** ►

Brothers, now your friends have come!
Be brave! Be brave!
Would you see me taken captive?

Moving Robe Woman's War Song

With the arrival of more agency families, Sitting Bull's camp had swelled to some seven thousand people. Because game, firewood, and forage were needed in vast amounts, it was time to be on the move again. A new site for the huge encampment was along the western bank of the Little Bighorn River. The Sioux called the river the Greasy Grass because their ponies grew strong and fat on its nourishing grasses.

A warrior's wife, Pretty White Cow, described the picturesque setting: "The country was good; there was rich grass for the ponies, and sweet water; the fields glowed with prairie flowers of yellow and red and blue; there were buffaloes in the valleys and Indian turnips on the hills for digging."

Sitting Bull and his Hunkpapas set up their tipis at the southern end of the camp that stretched along the river for three miles. The Cheyennes were assigned to the northern end. "In the camping as well as in the traveling, the Cheyennes and the Uncpapas (Hunkpapas) occupied the specially exposed positions," Wooden Leg said. The other tribes were circled in between, with each tribal circle in its appointed position and each tipi in its appointed place within its own tribal circle.

After four days of mourning for the twenty-one warriors who had been killed in the Fight with Three Stars, the camp held a joyous, singing–dancing victory celebration. Sitting Bull had a double reason to celebrate. His wife Four Robes had given birth to twin sons only a few weeks before.

Even though Sitting Bull had some eighteen hundred zealous young warriors raring to fight, he knew that more was needed than sheer numbers. Prayer was needed. Just before sundown on June 24, he crossed the Greasy Grass with One Bull at his side. Climbing a high ridge, they had a spectacular view to the west of the snow-capped Bighorn Mountains. Thousands of ponies grazed on the plains west of camp as smoke from the tipi fires curled into the evening sky. Muted sounds rose in the still summer air: the pulsing beat of drums, singing, heralds crying out the news, mothers calling to their children, dogs barking.

This was Sitting Bull's world as he had always known it. This was the world that he must keep free for his people. Heavily painted, with his long hair loose, Sitting Bull offered gifts to Wakan Tanka: a pipe, a buffalo robe, and tobacco.

"Great Spirit, pity me," he chanted. "In the name of the nation, I offer you this peace-pipe. Wherever, the sun, the moon, the earth, the four points of the winds, there you are always.

Save the Tribe, I beg you. Pity me, we wish to live. Guard us against all misfortunes or calamities. Pity me."

The very next afternoon, on a hot and dusty June 25, 1876, criers in every camp circle heralded an attack: "The chargers are coming! They are charging! The chargers are coming!"

Long Knives had ridden in from the east and were falling into camp, just as Sitting Bull had foreseen in his vision. They had already crossed the Greasy Grass and were firing on the Hunkpapa circle of tipis. All was confusion as the warriors rushed for their weapons, war paint, and horses. But first, always first, they had to make sure that the women, children, and old ones were safe.

After mounting his black warhorse with white stockings, Sitting Bull pulled his mother up behind him and rode hard for the northern Cheyenne end of camp. The rest of his family fled north on their own, with Four Robes carrying one of her twin sons. But when someone asked Four Robes where the other twin was, she realized that in her panic, she had left him behind. Racing back, she swept up her baby and rode him to safety with the others. One twin boy became known as Fled-With, while the other was called Fled-and-Abandoned.

With no time to paint or dress for war, Sitting Bull galloped back to the Hunkpapa circle. "Be brave, boys. It will be a hard time—brave up!" he shouted to the warriors who were riding to the scene.

Neither Sitting Bull nor anyone else realized that these Long Knives were the hated Seventh Cavalry commanded by Long Hair Custer. Dividing up his regiment, Custer had ordered Major Marcus Reno and 175 men to cross the Little Bighorn

River and strike at the southern end of the village. Captain Frederick Benteen, with 125 men, was to scout to the left for more Sioux. Custer himself would lead five companies along the bluffs in an attack on the tipi circles to the north. The supply train lagged far to the rear.

Moving Robe Woman, the daughter of Sitting Bull's friend Crawler, described the chaos: "I heard a terrific volley of carbines. The bullets shattered the tipi poles. Women and children were running away from the gunfire. In the tumult I heard old men and women singing death songs for their warriors who were now ready to attack the soldiers. The enchanting death songs made me brave, although I was a woman."

Moving Robe Woman's brother was killed in the Long Knives' opening charge. "My heart was bad. Revenge! Revenge!" she vowed. "I painted my face with crimson and braided my black hair. I was mourning. I was a woman, but I was not afraid . . . Father led my black horse up to me and I mounted. We galloped towards the soldiers."

More and more warriors joined the Hunkpapas, including Crazy Horse, who came racing through the village at the head of his Oglalas. The soldiers, who had dismounted, panicked at the size and ferocity of the war party. They turned and ran for their own horses, which they had left behind in the cottonwood groves near the river.

Now, as the warriors raced their horses back and forth to give them a second wind before the battle, the soldiers mounted and tried to cross the swift river to safety on the other side. But the warriors were all over them, shooting them full of arrows and knocking them from their horses with war clubs and gun barrels. The twenty-three-year-old Moving Robe Woman was in the forefront of the action. Years later, a Hunkpapa warrior remembered her well. "Holding her brother's war staff over her head, and leaning forward upon her charger, she looked as pretty as a bird."

Those soldiers who managed to make it across the river stampeded up the hill to a high treeless bluff. Forty had been killed, thirteen wounded, and sixteen left behind in the cotton-woods, not a good place to be. The women and young boys were going among the dead and wounded, killing those who were still alive. Despite Sitting Bull's warning, they stripped the soldiers' bodies of clothing and possessions.

An Army interpreter who was married to a Hunkpapa woman was among the wounded. He was a black man, known to the Sioux as Teat. "My friends, you have already killed me; don't count coup on me," he begged.

Overhearing his plea and sympathizing, Sitting Bull dismounted. "Don't kill that man; he is a friend of mine," he ordered as he gave Teat a drink of water. But as soon as Sitting Bull had forded the Greasy Grass to the other side, an angry woman shot and killed the man she called a traitor.

After Sitting Bull crossed the river, he rode for the bluff where Reno's men had taken up a defensive position. He didn't join in the fighting but stayed to one side, directing the others. Now a more serious threat loomed to the north. Long Hair Custer and his battalion of 210 men were seen riding along the bluff toward the northern end of camp.

Even though the soldiers were on the other side of the river, the northern end was where the women and children had gathered. With Crazy Horse leading the charge, the warriors turned away from a sure victory over Reno's men and headed north to defend the helpless ones from a possible attack.

Suddenly a company of Long Knives broke off from Custer's battalion. Mounted on gray horses, they headed down a ravine opposite the Sans Arc and Miniconjou circles at a place where the Greasy Grass could easily be forded. An enraged Gall took the lead against them. The Long Knives had killed his two wives and three children in their opening attack on the Hunkpapa tipis.

"It made my heart bad," Gall said about the deaths. "After that I killed all my enemies with the hatchet."

War whooping, yelping, and blowing their eagle-bone whistles, Gall and his Hunkpapas plunged their horses into the river and swam across. They scattered the terror-stricken soldiers, shooting them down as they tried to scramble back up the treeless hillside to rejoin their comrades.

As soon as they saw the pony soldiers riding along the bluffs toward the north, the old men and boys moved the women and children a half mile farther out on the plains. But even there they were vulnerable to attack. Insisting that One Bull join him, Sitting Bull rode north to stand guard over the helpless ones. Mounted on his warhorse, he strained to watch the distant battle through the lowering haze of gunsmoke and dust.

By now Crazy Horse and his Oglalas, with Two Moon and his Cheyennes, were mixing it up with Long Hair's pony soldiers on the bluffs. It was close to where Sitting Bull had offered his prayers and gifts to Wakan Tanka the night before.

Standing Bear described the heat of battle: "Everywhere our warriors began yelling: *'Hoka hey!* Hurry! Hurry!' It got dark

104

with dust and smoke. I could see warriors flying all around me like shadows, and the noise of all those hoofs and guns and cries was so loud it seemed quiet in there and the voices seemed to be on top of the cloud."

Pretty White Cow tried to watch the battle from across the river. "The smoke of the shooting and the dust of the horses shut out the hill," she said. "The soldiers fired many shots, but the Sioux shot straight and the soldiers fell dead."

It was true. Within a little more than an hour, the bodies of Long Hair Custer and five companies of the Seventh Cavalry lay sprawled all over the hillside. No one had recognized Custer. He had grown a new beard and his hair had been cut short.

Iron Hawk summed up the action: "These *Wasichus* wanted it, and they came to get it, and we gave it to them."

Sitting Bull was more compassionate. "My heart is full of sorrow that so many were killed on each side, but when they compel us to fight, we must fight."

As the women and boys crossed the Greasy Grass to plunder and mutilate the bodies, the warriors rode four miles south to finish off Reno's men. But Benteen's battalion and the packers with the supply train had joined them. In a hastily thrown-together fortification they were able to hold off their attackers.

That evening Sitting Bull returned to the bluff with White Bull and others to fire on the soldiers. Although a number of warriors stayed through the night to prevent the soldiers from escaping, Sitting Bull headed back to camp to help with the wounded and mourn the dead. Perhaps he mourned, too, that his people had stripped and robbed the bodies against his counsel.

The next day Sitting Bull again rode to the bluff, where the

350 survivors of the Seventh Cavalry had dug in even deeper. With more than 260 Long Knives dead, Sitting Bull ordered an end to the fighting.

"This is not my doings, nor these men's," he declared. "They are fighting because they were commanded to fight. We have killed their leader. Let them go. I call on the Great Spirit to witness what I say. We did not want to fight . . . we had to defend our wives and children."

By evening the whole camp was on the move west toward the Bighorn Mountains. After the traditional four days of mourning for the more than forty Sioux and Cheyenne deaths, the people celebrated the stunning victory that gave the year 1876 its Hunkpapa name, "Long-Hair-Killed."

Crazy Horse had played a key role in defending the Sioux and Cheyenne village. Gall, Two Moon, White Bull, Moving Robe Woman, and hundreds and hundreds of brave warriors had, too. It was true that Sitting Bull had taken part in the fight only when the Hunkpapa circle had been threatened. But it was Sitting Bull's prayers, songs, speeches, thoughtful counsel, and especially his deep-seated mystical strength and religious spirit that had lifted up his people and united them into an unstoppable force.

◄ **20** ►

Friends, whenever you pursue anything
Friend, may I be there.

Hunkpapa War Song

Sitting Bull's greatest regret at what the Sioux called the "Fight When Long Hair Did Not Go Home" was that his people hadn't listened to him. They had stripped the Long Knives of their clothing and possessions. Years afterward One Bull still remembered Sitting Bull's warning: "He told the people that they should not set their hearts on any thing or things the white people had or it would be a curse on them."

The Hunkpapa warrior Moving Robe Woman agreed. "After the battle the Indians took all the equipment and horses belonging to the soldiers," she said. "The brave men (the soldiers) who came to punish us that morning were defeated but in the end the Indians lost."

Despite the greatest victory that the Indians had ever known, they did indeed lose in the end. They had killed Custer and his men on June 25, 1876, only nine days before the United States joyfully prepared to celebrate the one-hundredth anniversary of the Declaration of Independence. Outraged citizens never saw the similarity between their fight for independence and the Plains tribes' fight for their independence . . . and survival. Nor did they understand that the Sioux and Cheyennes were defending their village against Custer's attack. With the nation demanding revenge, the military was at last given everything that it wanted: more money, more troops, more forts.

Still savoring their defeat of Three Stars Crook and Long Hair Custer, the tribes broke camp in the Bighorn Mountains and went their separate ways. Sitting Bull led his Hunkpapas, as well as some Miniconjous and Sans Arcs, east to Killdeer Mountain. Crazy Horse traveled to Paha Sapa with his Oglalas, while many of the others headed back to their agencies.

One hot day in August 1876, not long after the big village disbanded, Johnny Bruguier appeared in Sitting Bull's camp seeking refuge. A small, dark man of mixed Sioux and white heritage, Bruguier had been an interpreter at Standing Rock Agency. Now he was wanted for murder by the white authorities.

Suspicious of strangers as always, the Hunkpapa warriors talked of killing him. But the generous-hearted Sitting Bull took Johnny Bruguier into his tipi, just as he had taken in Jumping Bull and Frank Grouard. As Sitting Bull talked to Johnny, the people gathered outside and peered under the rolled-up sides of his tipi, trying to listen.

"Well, if you are going to kill this man, kill him," Sitting Bull called out, "and if you are not, give him a drink of water, something to eat, and a pipe of peace to smoke."

Certainly no one was foolish enough to kill a guest in Sitting Bull's tipi. From then on, Johnny Bruguier had free run of the camp on the fine horse that Sitting Bull gave him. Because he wore wide-winged chaps that flapped about his legs, the Hunkpapas called him Big Leggings.

Meanwhile, Three Stars Crook, with two thousand men, was marching around the countryside north of the Black Hills in torrential rains, searching for the killers of Custer. Because they were desperately short of rations and supplies, Three Stars ordered Captain Anson Mills and his command of 150 men to head for the Black Hills to pick up provisions.

Sitting Bull's onetime friend and now archenemy, Frank Grouard, the Grabber, was still scouting for the Army. Accompanying Mills and his men on their way to the Black Hills, the Grabber followed a trail that led to a Miniconjou village of thirty-seven lodges, near Slim Buttes. In what seemed to have become standard Army procedure, on September 9, 1876, Mills and his troops attacked the sleeping camp just before dawn. As the Miniconjou families tried to escape from their tipis, which they had fastened down against the rain, the Long Knives slaughtered them. Those who survived took shelter in a nearby rocky ravine or fled to the surrounding craggy granite buttes.

By chance Sitting Bull had come down from Killdeer Mountain and was camped about thirty miles away. He was once again in mourning for a beloved child. Only days before, his young son had been killed when a mule had kicked him in the head. Death of a brave warrior on the battlefield was somehow bearable. Death of an innocent child was not. As Sitting Bull began the mourning rites, he anguished over his devastating loss.

Nevertheless, when a runner arrived with news of the Slim Buttes massacre, he donned his buffalo-horn headdress with its long feather tail and assembled a war party. He couldn't save his own son but maybe he could save someone else's child. Besides, these Miniconjous were his friends. They had ridden with him into battle, and now they were in trouble.

After reaching Slim Buttes, Sitting Bull and his war party made their way around the back of the rocky cliffs and joined the Miniconjou warriors who were shooting down on the Long Knives. Crazy Horse and his Oglalas, who had also answered the call for help, were already there.

But Three Stars Crook had been alerted, too. He and his main body of men arrived at about eleven o'clock to reinforce Mills. Until late afternoon the two sides exchanged gunfire in an ever-thickening cloud of gunsmoke. But after weeks of marching in rain and mud and eating their horses to ward off starvation, the Long Knives were in no mood for a prolonged fight.

After scattering the Miniconjous' pony herds, Three Stars' men set fire to the village and all the people's food stores and belongings. They then headed south for the Black Hills in the pouring rain. Sitting Bull and the warriors harassed them for a short while and then let them go.

The Battle of Slim Buttes marked a turning point. Fresh from their two victories, Sitting Bull and his Hunkpapas had counted on having seen the last of the Long Knives. Now the Battle of Slim Buttes brought them up short. The *Wasichus* hadn't fled after all. Instead, they were overrunning the countryside with more determination and in greater numbers than ever. Although plundering the bodies of Long Hair's men may not have brought a curse on his people, it might have been hard to convince Sitting Bull otherwise.

·21·

All over the earth I roam,
All alone I've wandered,
Love of my country
Is the reason I'm doing this.

Sitting Bull's
Song of Despair

With the Battle of Slim Buttes, the Army's summer campaign was over, and the Black Hills still legally belonged to the Sioux. The government had tried to buy the Black Hills and failed. Waging war against the Sioux had failed, too. There was nothing left to do but take the land by blackmail.

Knowing how eager the country was to get its hands on the gold-rich Black Hills, Congress made an announcement. No more food would be distributed at any of the agencies until the agency chiefs signed a new treaty. Under the new treaty, the Sioux would turn over to the government both the Black Hills and the millions of acres of their prime hunting grounds known as the "unceded Indian territory." This time no mention was made of the 1868 Fort Laramie Treaty, which required that three-quarters of all adult Indian males agree to any loss of their land.

Blackmail worked. Faced with the starvation of their people, the agency chiefs had no choice but to sign the treaty in September 1876. One grieving chief covered his eyes with a blanket as he made his mark.

Control of the agencies was also shifted from the Indian Bureau in the Department of the Interior to the War Department. Under military rule, those Sioux living on agencies became official prisoners of war and had to surrender their horses and firearms. Sitting Bull, Crazy Horse, and everyone else still out were considered to be trespassing on government property. The War Department ordered the Army to forcibly drive them onto the Great Sioux Reservation, where they would be settled on agencies.

Of course Sitting Bull had never signed any treaty, new or old. This was the land that gave him life and from which he drew his strength. He often walked barefoot in the damp grass of early dawn to "hear the very heart of the Holy Earth." Under no circumstances would he ever leave or give up any part of it.

It was clear, however, that the Army wasn't going to give up either. Colonel Nelson Miles, who was known as Bear Coat because of the bearskin cap and fur-trimmed coat he wore, was in charge of a new Army fort going up at the confluence of the Tongue and Yellowstone rivers. But this was the Sioux' primary hunting ground, the land that they had wrested from the Crows. Now the Army was frightening away all the buffalo. Peace-minded Miniconjou and Sans Arc chiefs urged Sitting Bull to parley with Bear Coat.

But Sitting Bull, who was still in mourning for his son, was certain that no good could come of a meeting and he refused.

113

Instead he had Big Leggings Bruguier write a letter for him, which he left where Bear Coat was sure to find it.

> I want to know what you are doing traveling on this road. You scare all the buffalo away. I want to hunt in this place. I want you to turn back from here. If you don't, I will fight you again. I want you to leave what you have got here, and turn back from here. I am your friend,
>
> Sitting Bull
>
> I mean all the rations you have got and some powder. Wish you would write as soon as you can.

When there was no reply, the Miniconjou and Sans Arc chiefs again pressed Sitting Bull to parley with Bear Coat. Finally, on October 20, 1876, Sitting Bull reluctantly met with Miles north of the Yellowstone River, near Cedar Creek. Some six hundred warriors lined the ridges and ledges overlooking the meeting place. An equal number of Miles's command gathered in formation on a ridge directly opposite. Each side was poised for war in case the council turned stormy.

With Big Leggings interpreting, Sitting Bull and Bear Coat exchanged angry accusations and charges against each other for two days. Sitting Bull, still in his threadbare mourning clothes, made it clear that he wanted all the whites off the land and the forts abandoned.

In turn, Bear Coat Miles ordered Sitting Bull and his Hunk-papas to surrender unconditionally, move onto the Great Sioux Reservation, and live at an agency. If they didn't, he would attack them. With that, the conference broke up and the soldiers moved in for battle.

The warriors fought back as they covered the retreat of their women and children. With the Long Knives in pursuit, they set the dry prairie grass on fire to slow the soldiers' advance. Although the Army claimed a victory at what it called the Battle of Cedar Creek, it was hardly a battle. One warrior was killed and two soldiers were wounded before Sitting Bull led his Hunkpapas to safety.

The fierce Plains winter soon set in, but instead of withdrawing into their forts as they usually did, the soldiers kept up the pressure. At dawn on November 25, 1876, Three Stars Crook and his men attacked and burned Dull Knife and Little Wolf's Cheyenne village in the Bighorn Mountains, killing forty men, women, and children. Of those who fled, eleven babies died of cold and exposure, while many survivors suffered frozen limbs.

Black Elk recalled those desperate times: "Wherever we went, the soldiers came to kill us."

Bear Coat Miles was relentless in his pursuit of Sitting Bull and the Hunkpapas. He followed their trail and skirmished with them when he could, and when he couldn't, he harassed them. He plundered their food supplies and forced them to pack up and move on again and again in sub-zero weather.

During December, Bear Coat met with Big Leggings Bruguier at the Fort Peck trading post. By promising to clear his name of murder charges, he persuaded Big Leggings to leave Sitting Bull and become a scout for the Army. Once again Sitting Bull had to admit that his generosity had led him astray. If he ever saw Big Leggings again, he would kill him.

But for now, Sitting Bull had to bolster up his people. With their families and horses starving, more and more of his followers argued for peace. And more and more Miniconjous, Sans Arcs, and even Hunkpapas were surrendering to the agencies, including his nephew White Bull. Sitting Bull's cousin Black Moon and fifty-two Hunkpapa lodges crossed the northern border to live in Canada. Sitting Bull, who found himself increasingly isolated, sang of his despair.

> *"All over the earth I roam,*
> *All alone I've wandered,*
> *Love of my country*
> *Is the reason I'm doing this."*

As that bitter winter witnessed more deadly skirmishes and more defections, Sitting Bull spent a great deal of time in thought. He had to come to a decision and he wanted to be sure that it was the right one. Finally, in January, he made up his mind. The welfare of his Hunkpapas had to come first. He would lead his family and his people to safety in Canada, called the Land of the Grandmother in honor of Great Britain's Queen Victoria.

When Sitting Bull delivered fifty boxes of ammunition to Crazy Horse later that month, he urged his Oglala friend to join him and his Hunkpapas.

"We can find peace in the Land of the Grandmother," he pointed out. "We can sleep sound there, our women and children can lie down and feel safe."

But Crazy Horse turned him down.

In March, Sitting Bull and his Hunkpapa band were camped north of the Fort Peck trading post when the Missouri River flooded, destroying many of their tipis and nearly all of their belongings. Their possessions down to bare bones, they continued north, always north. In April Sitting Bull met with Miniconjou and Sans Arc head chiefs. He announced that although he would rather have fought on, he intended to travel to the Land of the Grandmother with his people.

And he did. During the first week in May 1877, Sitting Bull and some one thousand exhausted followers crossed the sacred road. They were in Canada. It was the same week that Crazy Horse and nearly nine hundred Oglalas surrendered at Camp Robinson. It was the same week that Bear Coat Miles killed the Miniconjou chief Lame Deer and destroyed his village, thereby crushing the last Sioux holdouts.

With what regrets Sitting Bull and his people traveled past the rock cairns that marked the Canadian border can only be imagined. But unlike their fellow Sioux in the United States, they were still alive . . . and free.

‣ 22 ‣

Only One, Only One, loved by everyone,
Only One speaks sweet words to everyone,
Hence the Only One loved by everyone.

Sitting Bull's Song to His Children

Sitting Bull, his family, and his one thousand followers set up camp some forty miles north of the Canadian border on high ground, west of Wood Mountain, near Pinto Horse Butte. They were hungry, tired, and ragged. Sitting Bull looked as shabby, if not shabbier, than anyone else. He once said, "My people look up to me because I am poor." And well they might. After the flood had destroyed their camp in March, Sitting Bull shared everything he had with the needy and helpless ones.

The Sioux had hardly arrived when the commander of Fort Walsh, Major James M. Walsh of the North-West Mounted Police, rode up with six other officers. Wearing the official red jacket and tall white helmet of the newly formed Mounted Police, Walsh met with Sitting Bull. After Sitting Bull had run through all his complaints against the United States, Walsh

118

welcomed him and his people to the Land of the Grandmother.

Although Canada would provide them with neither land nor rations, Walsh explained, they would be protected by her laws. Furthermore, no American soldiers would be allowed to follow them over the border. On the other hand, if the Sioux broke the law or returned to the United States to steal horses or fight, then Canada could no longer protect them. The choice was theirs.

Just as Walsh and his men were about to leave, a warrior rode into camp, leading stolen horses. Walsh didn't hesitate. Knowing full well that his little force wouldn't have a chance against the hundreds of warriors who surrounded them, he had his men arrest the thief.

Sitting Bull was impressed. Here was his own kind of man, someone who fearlessly enforced the rules he set down. If Sitting Bull had been told that one day he would trust and respect a *Wasichu* in uniform, he probably would have laughed. But over time, he formed a strong friendship with Walsh, whom the Hunkpapas came to call Long Lance because of the long lances that he and his men carried on parade. With the red-jacketed Mounted Police an everyday presence, the Hunkpapas named the year 1877 "Red-Coats-Assemble."

Buffalo were plentiful that summer of 1877, and both the hunting and trading were good. Jean Louis Legaré, a French-Canadian who ran a nearby trading post, traded honest-weight goods for the Hunkpapas' robes and pelts. Gradually the concern that Bear Coat Miles would pursue them over the sacred road faded.

For the first time in years, Sitting Bull's people lived without fear. Her-Holy-Door, who no longer had to fret about her warrior-son's safety, was now able to enjoy her grandchildren in peace. Sitting Bull had time to enjoy his children, too. Putting his youngest ones on his back, he playfully trotted around camp, singing to them.

Sitting Bull and his Hunkpapas may have been well pleased to have left the United States behind, but their presence in Canada was causing friction between the two countries. The Canadian government worried that if buffalo became scarce, warfare might break out between the Sioux and the native Canadian tribes. Maybe, Canada suggested, the United States would allow the Sioux to keep their guns and horses if they agreed to surrender.

The United States government flatly refused. Although Bear Coat Miles itched for Sitting Bull's return so that he could whip him in battle, the government was perfectly satisfied to be rid of its number one nuisance. For their part, United States officials recommended that Canada treat the Sioux as Canadian Indians and allot them both land and rations.

The American proposal was about as appealing to Canada as the Canadian proposal had been to the Americans. Nevertheless, to show good faith, in October 1877 a three-man commission from Washington arrived in Canada to try and talk Sitting Bull and his followers into surrendering.

Their timing couldn't have been worse. Sitting Bull's nine-year-old son had just died after an illness. Sitting Bull had now lost three sons, two within less than a year. It didn't seem possible that he had to once again endure the agonizing rites of mourning for yet another child. Sitting Bull was also mourn-

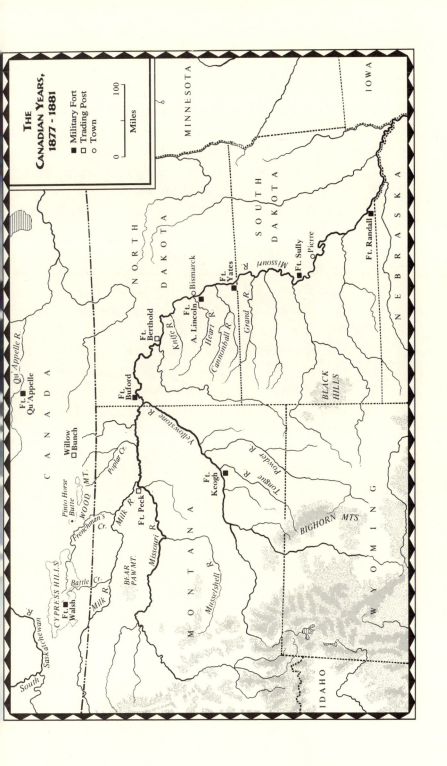

THE
CANADIAN YEARS,
1877 - 1881

■ Military Fort
□ Trading Post
○ Town

0 _____ 100
Miles

CANADA

Qu'Appelle R.
□ Ft. Qu'Appelle
□ Qu'Appelle

Willow □ Bunch

Pinto Horse • Butte WOOD MT.
Poplar Cr.

CYPRESS HILLS
■ Ft. Walsh
Battle Cr.
Frenchman's Cr.
BEAR PAW MT.
Milk R.
Milk R.
Missouri R.
□ Ft. Peck

M O N T A N A

Musselshell R.

Yellowstone R.

■ Ft. Keogh
Tongue R.
Powder R.

BIGHORN MTS

I D A H O

W Y O M I N G

N O R T H   D A K O T A

□ Ft. Berthold
Knife R.
■ Ft. A. Lincoln
Heart R.
○ Bismarck
■ Ft. Yates
Cannonball R.

■ Ft. Buford

S O U T H   D A K O T A

Grand R.
Missouri
■ Ft. Sully
○ Pierre

BLACK HILLS

■ Ft. Randall

M I N N E S O T A

I O W A

N E B R A S K A

South Saskatchewan R.

ing his good friend Crazy Horse. He had just gotten word that Crazy Horse had been murdered at Camp Robinson on September 5, bayoneted in the back by a soldier.

Sitting Bull was astonished that the American commission thought that he would consider surrendering when in all likelihood Crazy Horse's fate awaited him. He couldn't afford to take the risk. With the death of his son, his family needed him more than ever.

Although Sitting Bull was continually urged by Long Lance Walsh to meet with the Americans, his resistance hardened with the arrival of a band of Nez Percés. Rather than live on a government reservation in Idaho, eight hundred Nez Percés had fled into Montana with the intention of seeking refuge in Canada. On September 30, 1877, Bear Coat Miles had defeated them in a battle at Bear Paw Mountain. Bear Coat Miles again!

With many of the Nez Percés wounded and starving, the survivors had struggled north to Sitting Bull's camp. The Sioux and the Nez Percé were traditional enemies, but now Sitting Bull greeted them warmly, offering them food and shelter.

"You are welcome," he said. "You can stay as long as you please."

Sitting Bull pointed out the fate of the Nez Percés to Long Lance Walsh as an example of the American Army's brutality. "You see these men, women and children wounded and bleeding?" he asked. "We cannot talk to men who have blood on their hands."

But Long Lance persisted. Finally, as a favor to his new friend, Sitting Bull agreed. Accompanied by Walsh and twenty chiefs, Sitting Bull entered the Fort Walsh council room on

October 17. No longer in mourning, he wore a black-and-white calico shirt, black leggings, handsome embroidered moccasins, and a fox-skin cap.

Although he shook hands with all the Canadian redcoats, he pointedly ignored the Americans. He especially ignored the head of the commission, General Alfred One Star Terry, who had been Long Hair Custer's commanding officer. Every Sioux council began with the ritual smoking of a pipe, but as the ultimate insult, Sitting Bull and his chiefs allowed the meeting to open without a pipe ceremony.

One Star Terry spoke first. It was the same old story. When Sitting Bull and the Hunkpapas came into an agency, they would have to surrender their guns and their horses, which would then be sold to buy them livestock. The government would provide them with rations and clothing and treat them kindly.

Sitting Bull hadn't lost his sense of humor, and he grinned at the mention of "kindly treatment." Perhaps he would receive the same kindly treatment that Crazy Horse had received.

Sitting Bull spoke next, and he spoke from the heart. "We did not give you our country; you took it from us," he told the Americans after he had listed all the grievances that he held against them. "Look at these eyes and ears; you think me a fool; but you are a greater fool than I am," he said. "I have now come here to stay with these people, and I intend to stay here."

Those who had accompanied Sitting Bull also expressed themselves emotionally, including a woman, The-One-That-Speaks-Once. "I was over in your country; I wanted to raise my children over there, but you did not give me any time. I came

123

over to this country to raise my children and have a little peace," she said, ending with a suggestion that met with all the Hunkpapas' approval. "I want you to go back where you came from."

Two American reporters were at the council, and Sitting Bull agreed to give them an interview. For the first time, Americans could read in their newspapers words spoken by the infamous "killer of Custer." One of the reporters, who was somewhat of an artist, sketched Sitting Bull in his fox-skin cap so that Americans could see what he looked like as well.

Although Sitting Bull and his chiefs left the council sure that they had humiliated One Star, the Americans were well pleased. No one could accuse them of not doing their best to get Sitting Bull to surrender. No doubt Sitting Bull would have been surprised to learn that it was the Canadians who were taken aback. They now realized that they had been so welcoming that Sitting Bull and his people had no intention of ever leaving.

And to the Canadians' dismay, Sitting Bull's camp was growing larger almost daily. After Crazy Horse's murder, many Oglalas left the agencies and fled north to join Sitting Bull. When the Indian Bureau announced that both the Red Cloud and Spotted Tail agencies would be moved to the Missouri River, more unhappy Sioux arrived. By the spring of 1878, there were about five thousand people camped with Sitting Bull, including the Nez Percés. Although "Nez-Percés-Visit" was the name the Hunkpapas gave the year 1878, the Nez Percés' visit turned out to be permanent.

As Sitting Bull became a magnet for every dissatisfied Sioux, the Canadian government grew more and more alarmed. It took enormous quantities of game to sustain so many people, and in the summer of 1878 the great buffalo herds began to split up and drift south across the sacred road into the United States. The native Canadian tribes, especially the Blackfeet, were furious. These outsiders were killing off the buffalo that belonged in their cooking pots.

Sitting Bull was aware that if fighting broke out between the native Blackfeet and his people, the Sioux might well be expelled from the Land of the Grandmother. Statesman that he was, Sitting Bull extended his hand in a show of good will to Crow Foot, the head war chief of the Blackfeet. Meeting in council, the two men smoked the pipe of peace and pledged to end warfare and horse-stealing between them. In honor of their new relationship, Sitting Bull's twin son who had been known as Fled-and-Abandoned was now named Crow Foot by his father.

If Sitting Bull had hopes that his friendship pact with Crow Foot would satisfy the Canadian government, he was mistaken. But then Sitting Bull knew little about governments. All he knew was that he and his people had settled in the Land of the Grandmother and this was where they would stay. In the year that they had made their home across the sacred road, many children had been born.

"Are they not the children of the Grandmother?" he asked. "She will protect her children born on her soil, and she will protect the fathers and mothers of these children."

But Canada had other ideas, and so did the United States.

◄23►

The old men now so few
That they are not worth counting
I myself the last living
Therefore a hard time I am having.

Song of Famine

By 1879 game had become so scarce in the Land of the Grandmother that Sitting Bull and his Hunkpapas moved their hunting camps farther south, almost to the sacred road. From there they made quick runs into Montana to hunt buffalo.

"All I am looking for is something for my children to eat," Sitting Bull explained to Long Lance Walsh. "But I will not remain south of the line one day longer than I can help."

Even one day was too long for the Americans. They were already having trouble with Sitting Bull's unruly young warriors who continually crossed the border to steal horses and livestock as well as an occasional scalp. Furthermore, those tribes living on northern Montana agencies angrily complained that Sitting Bull's Sioux were coming down from Canada and making off with game that was rightfully theirs.

Exasperated by the continuing Sitting Bull problems, the Army granted Bear Coat Miles his wish. The next time Sitting Bull crossed into Montana, Bear Coat was ordered to drive him back into Canada.

In July 1879, Sitting Bull and six hundred of his people made a buffalo kill south of the border on Milk River. While most of the men returned north, Sitting Bull, Jumping Bull, and a number of others stayed behind to guard the women as they packed up the meat. Without warning, Bear Coat's advance command of eighty Crow scouts appeared. Quickly, the Hunkpapas spread out defensively so that the women and children could escape.

Magpie, a Crow chief, had often bragged that if he ever had the chance, he would personally rid the world of Sitting Bull. At Milk River, he had his chance. Astride his famous prized horse, Magpie challenged the forty-eight-year-old Sitting Bull to personal combat. Although the memory of his father's death in single combat might have momentarily given Sitting Bull pause, he accepted.

As the two men rode toward each other, Magpie got off the first shot. But his rifle misfired. Sitting Bull aimed, pulled the trigger, and blew off the top of Magpie's head. Dismounting, he limped over to the body, lifted what was left of Magpie's scalp, mounted Magpie's celebrated horse, and returned triumphantly to his own lines. Maybe now the Crows, and the *Wasichus* as well, would realize that it wasn't so easy to rid the world of Sitting Bull.

The Hunkpapa warriors who had already left hastily returned. But Bear Coat and his main force arrived, too, and the

Army howitzers dispersed the Hunkpapas in short order. Although the fight wasn't the great victory that Bear Coat later claimed that it was, it did serve to let Sitting Bull know that the blue-coated soldiers would no longer tolerate Sioux trespassers.

That fall buffalo were in shorter supply than ever. Raging wildfires that destroyed great expanses of grasslands were followed by winter blizzards. The frigid weather further weakened the hungry people and starving ponies.

Sitting Bull's situation had become like the Sioux game of "Throwing It In." Two boys would take turns at spinning tops into holes in the ice. If one boy spun his top into a hole and his opponent didn't, the loser had to give the winner his top. The game was over when one player lost all of his tops.

The year 1880 witnessed Sitting Bull losing most of his tops. Canada's once-warm welcome had turned chilly. The buffalo herds continued to thin out. Increasing numbers of families were heading south and going into agencies. Sitting Bull had once ordered the *akicita* to prevent anyone from leaving, but at the sight of so many sick and hungry children, he no longer had the heart to stop them. Even the spindly ponies suffered so severely from disease that the Hunkpapas called 1880 "Mange-Among-the-Horses."

Black Elk described how wretched their lives had become. "We began to feel homesick for our own country where we used to be happy," he mourned. "The old people talked much about it and the good days before trouble came. Sometimes I felt like crying when they did that."

Even Sitting Bull considered going in, although the thought

of surrendering at Fort Buford was especially painful. Of all the Army forts, Fort Buford, which had been built on the upper Missouri River in the heart of their buffalo country, was the one he hated most. Nevertheless, in May 1880 he sent One Bull down to Fort Buford to find out what would happen if he came in.

One Bull quoted Sitting Bull to the soldier chief: "I want to know what you will do with us if we will surrender. If it is good, I will come, if not, I won't. I will wait till the young man gets back. He represents my people."

Much as the Army wanted to get its hands on the legendary Sitting Bull, the officer gave the standard reply. Sitting Bull would be treated like everyone else. He must surrender unconditionally and turn over his arms and ponies. In return, he would be given rations and clothing.

Sitting Bull didn't decide anything in haste. This was one of the most difficult decisions he had ever made and he needed time to weigh both sides. He also wanted to counsel with those chiefs who were still with him.

"I was like a bird on the fence not knowing on what side to hop" was how he described his dilemma.

"Sitting Bull was a thinker and didn't take anything up until he thought it was good," Robert Higheagle later said. "He was for the Indians and was for protecting their rights."

It was an especially painful time for Sitting Bull. In November 1880, Jumping Bull, Black Moon, and his old friend Gall, along with 85 Hunkpapa lodges, rode south. Early in 1881 another old friend, Crow King, went in, taking 350 Hunkpapas with him.

Almost completely isolated, Sitting Bull was left with only his family, One Bull, his elderly uncle Four Horns, a few minor chiefs, and a number of women, children, and old men. In April he moved his camp thirty-five miles farther east to be closer to Willow Bunch, where his friend Jean Louis Legaré had relocated his trading post. Even though Legaré advised Sitting Bull to surrender, Sitting Bull knew that the trader was someone on whom he could count.

"I trust you, but not the Americans," Sitting Bull told him. "They are only waiting to get us all together, and then slaughter us."

Long Lance Walsh, of course, was the other man whom Sitting Bull trusted. However, knowing that Walsh was sympathetic to Sitting Bull, Canadian officials transferred Walsh to Fort Qu'Appelle. Even though the fort was 140 miles away, in May 1881 Sitting Bull decided to make the trip. He needed to talk over with Long Lance what he should do. Before he left, he told fellow warrior Old Bull to ride down to Fort Buford and learn how the people there were being treated.

With no game to be found, Sitting Bull and the 300 Hunkpapas who accompanied him to Fort Qu'Appelle were forced to eat gophers, roots, and what few ducks and fish they could catch. To Sitting Bull's dismay, when they arrived after a four-day journey, they discovered that Long Lance Walsh wasn't even there. To prevent a meeting between the two men, Canadian authorities had sent Walsh back east on an assignment.

Left with no choice, Sitting Bull had to deal with the Canadian Indian commissioner, Edgar Dewdney, who pushed, and pushed hard, for Sitting Bull to surrender. At the moment food, not surrender, was on Sitting Bull's mind. The people he had brought with him, including his favorite son, five-year-old Crow Foot, were starving.

"Now I beg of you to get some carts to go for some grub," he urged Dewdney. "I am wanting now two days some grub, so that the children might be eating."

Dewdney agreed to provide food, but only if Sitting Bull surrendered. Sitting Bull was mystified. "So long as one had food, all would have food" was the Sioux way. Yet here were the redcoats with an abundance of food who wouldn't give a bowl of soup to a hungry child. With nothing more to say, Sitting Bull and his people headed back to their encampment.

While Sitting Bull and the Hunkpapas had been gone, Old Bull had followed orders and ridden down to Fort Buford. Welcomed handsomely by the military, Old Bull had returned with a good report, so good that he and thirty-one Hunkpapas decided to go in. When Legaré went south to trade at Fort Buford, they traveled with him in his trading carts.

Sitting Bull's oldest daughter, Many Horses, also chose to surrender. Since the death of his third son, Sitting Bull had been especially protective of his surviving children. He had earlier refused a suitor's offer of ponies for Many Horses's hand in marriage. Now, while her father was away, Many Horses and the young man eloped in one of Legaré's carts.

With nothing gained from the Canadians, Sitting Bull arrived back at camp to find his cherished daughter gone, along with Old Bull and more Hunkpapa families. Heavy-hearted, he awaited Legaré's return. He had a proposal to make. If Legaré fed his people, he, Sitting Bull, would do anything that Legaré wanted.

Legaré agreed. After he put on a feast for the ravenous Hunkpapas, he said that he wanted Sitting Bull and the rest of his people to ride down to Fort Buford with him in two days' time and surrender.

Instead of living up to his promise, Sitting Bull hedged. "We cannot go as soon as that," he said. "Wait ten days, then maybe we shall be ready."

Legaré compromised. "I will wait seven days."

And so Sitting Bull smoked and thought, trying to see with the eyes in his heart. He loved his people and knew that they depended on him, especially his family, who had stood by him through the best and worst of circumstances. With the birth of a daughter in 1878 and another set of twin boys in 1880, more small, hungry faces looked up to him. At least if they went in, the children would be fed.

On the other hand, if he surrendered he might be jailed or even murdered, as Crazy Horse had been. Then what would happen to his loved ones? Agonizing as the decision was, in the end the survival of his family and his people won out. Sitting Bull made plans to surrender.

Thirty-five families chose to stay behind. The rest, 187 in all, climbed into Legaré's high-wheeled wooden carts and started off on July 12, 1881. Silent and somber, Sitting Bull rode beside them on his rib-thin pony as the caravan bumped along the rutted trail, leaving the Land of the Grandmother behind forever. All of Sitting Bull's tops had fallen through the holes in the ice. The game was over.

◄ 24 ►

A warrior I have been
Now it is all over.
A hard time I have.

Sitting Bull's
Song of Sorrow

On July 19, 1881, Sitting Bull's sad little cavalcade reached Fort Buford. Still carrying his Winchester, Sitting Bull wore a grimy, thin blanket around his waist, a dirty calico shirt, and patched black leggings. Bandages shaded his eyes, which were badly infected.

The formal surrender took place the next day. Sitting Bull was dressed in the same ragged clothes he had worn the day before. He was accompanied by his young son Crow Foot, Legaré, and thirty-two Hunkpapas, all the warriors still loyal to him from the thousands who had once followed him into battle. Silently, the proud war chief laid his Winchester on the floor between his feet.

With an interpreter, a reporter, and Army officers crowding the room, the commanding officer of Fort Buford opened the meeting. He told Sitting Bull that he and his people would travel by steamboat down the Missouri River to Standing Rock Agency in Dakota, where they would join the more than three thousand Sioux who were already there. As promised, he would be treated fairly, just as the others were being treated fairly.

Sitting Bull said nothing for long minutes. Then he gestured to Crow Foot, who picked up his father's Winchester and handed it to the soldier chief. Only then did Sitting Bull speak.

"I surrender this rifle to you through my young son, whom I now desire to teach in this way that he has become a friend of the whites," he told the commanding officer through the interpreter. "I wish him to live as the whites do and to be taught in their schools. I wish to be remembered as the last man of my tribe who gave up his rifle. This boy has now given it to you, and he wants to know how he is going to make a living."

The Army officers must have had some sense of Sitting Bull's pain and humiliation. This was, after all, the man whose warriors had defeated Crook and Custer and who had kept his people free four years after all the other Sioux had come in.

Apparently Sitting Bull didn't realize the seriousness of his situation. Rambling on with a list of demands, he still talked of hunting, trading, and living where he pleased.

None of it would ever happen.

On July 29 Sitting Bull and his handful of followers were herded aboard a steamboat for the trip down the Missouri River to Standing Rock Agency. Not only was the river passage aboard the fire-boat a first-time experience for Sitting Bull and his Hunkpapas, but so was their reception when they tied up at

134

Bismarck, Dakota, for a stopover. Several hundred townspeople gathered for a glimpse of the infamous "killer of Custer."

Unaware that his poverty was a mark of his generosity, the good citizens of Bismarck were disappointed with Sitting Bull's appearance. Rather than an exotic warbonnet and breechcloth, he wore threadbare pants and a dirty white shirt, with his three braids bound in red flannel and red paint streaking his neck, face, and the part in his hair.

That noon Sitting Bull, his family, and his headmen were escorted to the local hotel. Again, Bismarckers flocked to watch the war chief and his people eat with knives and forks for the first time. (They managed very well.) Sitting Bull handled the affair with his usual grace and humor. Delighted with the lavish banquet, he laughed mightily when the interpreter read off all the fancy names for the different courses. Most astonishing was the ice cream. Puzzled, Sitting Bull remarked that he "could not see how such stuff could be frozen in hot weather."

Sitting Bull had always been a fast learner. Taught to write his name by a white trader while in Canada, he now discovered that the *Wasichus* would pay for his signature as well as for Hunkpapa ornaments and knickknacks. When he boarded the steamboat for the sixty-mile trip to Standing Rock, coins jingled pleasantly in his pockets.

On August 1, 1881, Standing Rock Agency and Fort Yates, the military post that safeguarded the agency, swung into view along the high banks of the Missouri River. Hard as it may have been for Sitting Bull to imagine his life here, at least he would once again see those whom he cared about the most: his daughter Many Horses, Jumping Bull, Black Moon, Gall, Crow King, and others.

But Army officials were having second thoughts about allowing Sitting Bull to live at Standing Rock. They were concerned that he, his family, and his little band of mostly women, children, and old men would be a threat to the peaceful running of the agency. On the other hand, they had promised that when he surrendered he could live at Standing Rock. For a month the Army debated what to do.

It was a pleasant month for Sitting Bull and his followers. Their stay turned out to be so memorable that the Hunkpapas called 1881 "They-Stop-at-Standing-Rock-to-Camp." Setting up their tipis on the sandy shore of the Missouri River, they spent their time feasting, visiting friends and relatives, and talking over old times. And Sitting Bull had an emotional reunion with Many Horses, who left her husband and returned to her father's tipi. "We both cried. I was happy to see her," he declared.

But Sitting Bull was definitely not happy when the Army announced its decision. As prisoners of war, Sitting Bull, his family, and those who had traveled with him from the Land of the Grandmother were to be shipped down the Missouri River to Fort Randall on the Dakota and Nebraska border. Every American and Canadian official whom Sitting Bull had talked to during the past four years had guaranteed that if he surrendered, he and his people would be settled at Standing Rock. They had lied! Although Sitting Bull knew that he shouldn't be surprised at anything the Army did, he flew into a rage at this latest betrayal. He would rather die like Crazy Horse than be sent into exile.

Sitting Bull's understandable fury didn't impress the Army. On September 9, 1881, he, his family, and his followers, including the loyal One Bull, 167 Hunkpapas altogether, boarded a steamer for the trip down the river. Not only were they prodded up the gangway by foot soldiers with bayoneted rifles, but a company of soldiers guarded them the whole way.

On their arrival, Sitting Bull and his Hunkpapas set up their camp on the prairie, half a mile west of Fort Randall. Although they were unarmed and without horses, blue-coated soldiers constantly patrolled the pitiful little knot of thirty-two tipis. The Hunkpapas even had to make an appearance every morning for a head count.

Despite Sitting Bull's constant inquiries and pleas to be sent back to Standing Rock, the Army stood firm. Separated from friends and kinspeople and with nothing to do, the days seemed endless. In October an artist, Rudolf Cronau, called Iron Eyes because of his spectacles, visited Fort Randall. He had just left Standing Rock, where he had painted portraits of many of Sitting Bull's fellow warriors. When the portraits were displayed, Sitting Bull and his people were thrilled to see likenesses of their old comrades. During his stay, Iron Eyes, who struck up a friendship with Sitting Bull and One Bull, painted both their portraits.

In December a missionary arrived at Fort Randall with copies of fifty-five drawings that Sitting Bull had done for Jumping Bull back in 1870. Called pictographs, forty-one of the drawings portrayed Sitting Bull performing brave deeds, and fourteen depicted Jumping Bull's brave deeds. Astride his horse and holding his sacred shield in almost every drawing, Sitting Bull had also signed each one with his glyph. Naturally enough, his glyph was an image of a seated buffalo bull connected to the image of himself by a line, in the traditional Sioux fashion. The soldiers at Fort Randall were so taken with the pictographs that in 1882 Sitting Bull made more copies, although this time instead of a glyph he signed his name.

Sitting Bull's imprisonment at Fort Randall was difficult, as difficult a time as he had ever known. Constantly guarded by soldiers, unable to hunt or even ride, far from friends, dependent on Army rations and supplies, he was completely powerless for the first time in his life.

At least he had his family and little band of supporters. And he did strike up a friendship with a young officer, George Ahern. Taking an interest in Sitting Bull's children, Ahern suggested to Sitting Bull's ten-year-old daughter, Standing Holy, that she be sent away to a convent school. Standing Holy ran to her father's side and took his hand to await his decision. There was nothing to decide. He would never part with another child.

"No," he said. "I love you too much. Nothing but sorrow would come of it."

He had experienced enough sorrow of late. As always, Sitting Bull expressed himself best through song.

> *"A warrior I have been*
> *Now it is all over.*
> *A hard time I have."*

At last, after almost two years, the Secretary of War ordered Sitting Bull and the other Hunkpapa prisoners of war be sent back to Standing Rock Agency. There they would be under the supervision of the Bureau of Indian Affairs in the Department of the Interior. After more than twenty years, Sitting Bull would no longer be pursued, hunted down, shot at, or guarded by blue-coated soldiers. As far as he was concerned, it couldn't happen soon enough.

·25·

We're tenting tonight on the old campground.
Give us a song to cheer our weary hearts,
A song of home and friends we love so dear.
Many are the hearts that are weary tonight,
Wishing for the war to cease;
Many are the hearts that are looking for the right
To see the dawn of peace.

Buffalo Bill's Favorite Song

After twenty long months of imprisonment, Sitting Bull and his little band of Hunkpapas arrived by steamboat at Standing Rock Agency on May 10, 1883. The newcomers, who were overjoyed to see their relatives and friends again, set up their tipis a mile or so from the agency. The agency was a cluster of offices, shops, storehouse, council house, school, church, and other buildings, all close by Fort Yates.

Sitting Bull may have been powerless in captivity, but now that he was back among his own people, he would once again be supreme chief. The day after he arrived, he appeared in the office of James McLaughlin, the white Indian agent in charge of Standing Rock. He didn't want ration tickets, Sitting Bull told him. Instead, he was to receive all the rations and supplies, and as head chief, he would distribute them. He wasn't

140

going to put crops in this year, either, and by the way, he had appointed eleven chiefs and thirteen headmen.

It couldn't have been a worse beginning. McLaughlin told Sitting Bull in no uncertain terms that he was nothing special here at Standing Rock and he would be treated like everyone else. Furthermore, he would plant crops this spring as he was told.

Sitting Bull infuriated not only McLaughlin, but three months later he also managed to insult an entire commission of senators from Washington.

"I am here by the will of the Great Spirit and by his will I am chief," he announced. "If the Great Spirit has chosen anyone to be the chief of this country, it is myself."

When the commission chairman told Sitting Bull that he was no better than any other Indian, Sitting Bull retorted, "You have conducted yourselves like men who have been drinking whiskey, and I came here to give you some advice." With that, Sitting Bull waved his hand and every Hunkpapa in the room stood up and left. If either McLaughlin or the commission doubted that Sitting Bull was still head chief, he had just given them proof to the contrary.

At least Sitting Bull made amends the next day. "I am here to apologize to you for my bad conduct," he told the commissioners. But he didn't stay humble for long. "Of course," he added, "if a man is a chief, and has authority, he should be proud, and consider himself a great man."

It was just those qualities of authority, power, and chieftainship that McLaughlin was determined to tear down. He was an employee of the Indian Bureau, and it was the aim of the Indian Bureau to civilize, Christianize, and Americanize the Indians in their charge. They would become farmers, attend church, and send their children to school to learn "American" ways. And McLaughlin wasn't about to allow a defiant and arrogant Sitting Bull to stand in the way of his duty.

Everything was done to bring the Indians into line. Indian police forces, called *ceska maza,* or Metal Breasts in honor of their metal badges, were organized to keep order. Because the police forces were similar to the *akicita* societies, many one-time *akicita* warriors signed up. Indian courts were established to punish anyone who practiced ceremonies that were forbidden by the Indian Bureau. Indian Offenses, as they were called, included feasts, dances, certain medical and religious rituals, and just about everything that made an Indian an Indian. Fortunately, most of the time the courts weren't very strict.

Realizing that the old ways were gone forever, Sitting Bull's Strong Heart comrades and fellow warriors Gall and Crow King had begun to work with McLaughlin. Not so Sitting Bull. He had been chosen supreme chief of the Sioux Nation and he would continue to be supreme chief.

The hostility between Sitting Bull and McLaughlin didn't prevent McLaughlin from escorting Sitting Bull to Bismarck in October 1883. Bismarck, the new capital of the Dakota Territory, was planning a celebration. Now that Sitting Bull was a national celebrity, McLaughlin savored being known as the guardian of Custer's "killer." As for Sitting Bull, he was curious about this strange white world.

Wearing a stovepipe hat, Sitting Bull, as well as the other

Sioux guests, must have felt some sense of triumph. They marched in the grand parade ahead of former president Ulysses S. Grant, the president who had declared war on them seven years before.

It was all rather heady, and when McLaughlin traveled to St. Paul the following March, Sitting Bull asked to go along. During their two-week stay, Sitting Bull toured factories, mills, government offices, schools, and the firehouse. He was especially entertained by the firemen's instant and dramatic response to the jangle of their alarm.

Seeing what a public sensation Sitting Bull was, a St. Paul businessman put together a show called "The Sitting Bull Combination." Accompanied by an interpreter and McLaughlin's Dakota wife, Sitting Bull and five Hunkpapa companions traveled to twenty-five cities in September and October 1884.

The grand opening in St. Paul, starring Sitting Bull, was a smashing success. While an announcer described Indian life, Sitting Bull and his companions, who were wearing their most colorful finery and magnificent warbonnets, sat on the stage, smoking and cooking a meal in front of a tipi.

When The Sitting Bull Combination appeared in Philadelphia, a young Oglala, Standing Bear, who was a student at a nearby boarding school, came to a performance. Sitting Bull spoke in Lakota about the need for peace and education for his people. Standing Bear later reported that the interpreter translated the speech into a gory account of the Battle of the Little Bighorn.

"He told so many lies I had to smile," Standing Bear recalled. On the return trip west, Sitting Bull described the dancing-girl show he had seen in New York. Hilariously mimicking the dancing, he had everyone in the railroad car howling with laughter. The Indian Bureau didn't find Sitting Bull's presence at a dancing-girl show the least bit funny. Only reluctantly did the Bureau allow him to join Buffalo Bill Cody's Wild West show in June of the following year.

Sitting Bull's duties in the Wild West weren't strenuous. For $50 a week and a bonus of $125, he rode in the opening parade, appeared briefly in the arena, and greeted visitors at his tipi, where he sold photographs of himself. Ironically, Sitting Bull joined the show in Buffalo (New York), followed by a four-month tour in the United States and Canada. In the United States, Sitting Bull was usually booed as a villain, while in Canada he was greeted as a hero. Unconcerned about any *Wasichu*'s opinion, Sitting Bull didn't care one way or the other.

During the run of the Wild West, Sitting Bull and Buffalo Bill became close friends. Another good friend was the sharpshooter Annie Oakley. Sitting Bull dubbed her "Little Sure Shot" and inducted her into his tribe. Annie Oakley later observed that most of Sitting Bull's money "went into the pockets of small, ragged boys."

Although Sitting Bull enjoyed both his freedom and his new experiences, he never could understand the *Wasichus'* lack of generosity, especially toward needy children.

"The white man knows how to make everything," he observed, "but he does not know how to distribute it."

Before Sitting Bull returned to Standing Rock in October, Buffalo Bill presented him with two gifts that he always treasured, the light gray horse that he had ridden in the Wild West and a white sombrero. Buffalo Bill wanted Sitting Bull to star in his show the following year, but McLaughlin decided that Sitting Bull was growing a little too independent, a little too worldly, and a little too vain. With that, Sitting Bull's show business career was over.

It was true that in his travels, Sitting Bull had seen a lot and observed a lot, too. And he was never at a loss for words. When a reporter asked him what he thought of white people, he had a ready answer. "They are a great people," he said, "as numerous as the flies that follow the buffalo."

Humor aside, his more serious opinion was from the heart: "I would rather die an Indian than live a white man."

·26·

Great Spirit to earth He has sent me
Buffalo for food He has sent me
My mother to earth was she sent
Tribes with her was she sent.

Sitting Bull's Song
Dedicated to His Mother

As Sitting Bull settled down to life at Standing Rock Agency, a number of events caught him up short. In 1884 his mother, Her-Holy-Door, died after having been a much-loved member of his tipi since she had been widowed twenty-six years before. Everyone missed her wise counsel and good humor, none more than Sitting Bull. He couldn't remember a time when she hadn't loved, counseled, and supported him. That year also saw the death of Sitting Bull's childhood friend and loyal Hunkpapa chief Crow King, giving 1884 the name "Crow-King-Died."

Another event in 1884 brought back to Sitting Bull memories of his childhood. He and his family moved forty miles south of the agency to the Grand River, close by the place where he had been born. Earlier he had said to One Bull, "I was born at Many Caches, so we shall settle there."

146

On the south bank of the Grand River, the Place of Many Caches was where the Hunkpapas stockpiled their food in storage pits. The Grand River, which flowed through a deep, broad valley with groves of cottonwoods lining its banks, had always been one of their favorite camping sites. But because the river was flooded that spring, Sitting Bull and the some two hundred Hunkpapas who moved with him had to settle on the north bank instead.

Sitting Bull knew where he was born, but he was never sure of when. He once said, "Cannot tell exactly how old I am. We count our years from the moon between great events."

At least he was sure of when he had acquired his mystical power, or medicine. "I was still in my mother's insides when I began to study all about my people," he informed a reporter through an interpreter. "The God Almighty [Wakan Tanka] must have told me at that time that I would be the man to be the judge of all the other Indians—a big man, to decide for them in all their ways."

Four years after his arrival at Standing Rock, Sitting Bull still considered himself to be head chief of all his people. And although he may have left the white world behind, the white world, in the persons of two white women, came to him.

Mary Collins was a Protestant missionary at Standing Rock who became Sitting Bull's friend when she doctored his sick child. Calling each other "Sister" and "Brother," the two may have been friends, but they were also rivals for the spiritual well-being of the people.

The other woman was Catherine Weldon, who represented the National Indian Defense Association, an eastern organization sympathetic to the Indian cause. When she and her fourteen-year-old son arrived at Standing Rock in 1888, she made herself known to Sitting Bull. She showered him with gifts, wrote letters for him, and paid for feasts that he gave. Sitting Bull and Catherine, who was a widow in her thirties, soon became good friends.

But friends weren't family, and Sitting Bull always put his family first. His tipi circle now included his two wives, two stepsons, his daughter Standing Holy, two pairs of twin boys, the daughter who had been born in Canada, another son born in 1887, and a daughter born in 1888. His oldest daughter, Many Horses, was happily remarried.

Sadly, Sitting Bull's two staunchest supporters had died, his uncle Four Horns and his cousin Black Moon. Even more devastating was the sudden death of his daughter Walks Looking in 1887, leaving behind a husband, an infant son, and her grieving father. The whole Grand River community joined Sitting Bull in mourning his daughter's death. He had now buried four children, and it seemed as if each loss brought greater pain as memories of the others came echoing back.

The year 1888 brought pain of a different sort. The United States government was discussing plans to take over half of the Great Sioux Reservation for white settlement, some nine million acres.

Sitting Bull had seen enough of the white world to know that nothing had changed. No matter how much the *Wasichus* had, it was never enough. He had been told before he was born that he was a "big man" and that he was "to decide for other Indians in all their ways." And Sitting Bull decided that it was up to him to defend and protect what land was still left to his people.

He had lost three sons and a daughter and was determined to make sure that Sioux land would be kept safe for the children who were still left to him. And beyond them, their children and their children's children.

◀ 27 ▶

The tribe named me
So in courage
I shall live.

Sitting Bull's Song
to Rally the Sioux

Officials in Washington had wanted to break up the Great Sioux Reservation for years. As they saw it, only twenty thousand Sioux lived within the reservation. More than two hundred thousand whites lived around its edges, all of whom were clamoring for more land.

The government planned to cut six separate agencies out of the Great Sioux Reservation: Standing Rock, Pine Ridge, Rosebud, Cheyenne River, Lower Brulé, and Crow Creek. They all would be located in South Dakota except for a portion of Standing Rock, which extended into North Dakota.

The head of each Sioux family on the six agencies would be given one hundred and sixty acres of land, or smaller shares according to the size of the family. The land that was left over, almost half of the Great Sioux Reservation, would be turned over to white homesteaders for fifty cents an acre. The money would be payable to the Sioux when the homesteaders took up their claims.

Unlike its seizure of the Black Hills and the "unceded Indian territory," the government decided to make everything legal this time around. Three-quarters of all adult Sioux males would have to sign an agreement approving the sale of the land.

Sitting Bull had never signed away so much as an acre of land and he wasn't about to start now. He and his people had done everything that had been demanded of them. They had settled down peacefully, lived in log houses, sent their children to school, and raised crops and livestock. Still, the *Wasichus* continued to hover over Sioux land like vultures over a dying buffalo calf. Well, Sitting Bull wasn't dying and he wouldn't let his family or his people die either.

Three commissioners appeared at Standing Rock from Washington in July 1888 to persuade the Sioux to sign the agreement. Because everyone living at Standing Rock was opposed to selling the land, Sitting Bull didn't feel the need to speak out publicly. Perhaps realizing that he was a controversial figure, he worked behind the scenes, talking and advising in council. He also appointed four spokesmen to meet with the commission: Gall, John Grass, Mad Bear, and Big Head.

"Sitting Bull knew in silence there was wisdom," a family member later remarked.

During one of the council meetings, Black Bull, who was not known for his silence, told the commissioners that he had noticed how their people weighed everything before pricing it.

"You want to buy our land and we are willing to sell it at a fair price. I suggest that you bring here a big scale," he proposed. "We will weigh the earth and sell it to you by the pound."

The one or two times that Sitting Bull did appear in the council tent that had been set up near agency headquarters, he was calm and reasonable. "I want to know how many months you expect us to stay here," he politely asked the commissioners, "and by what time you will call it a decision."

After four weeks of coaxing and threatening, the commission finally called it a decision. Admitting defeat, they didn't even bother to visit the other agencies before returning to Washington.

Government officials, however, never gave up on something that they wanted, and they badly wanted the land. To woo the Sioux into signing the agreement, they invited Sitting Bull and sixty other chiefs to the Great Father's City for a visit.

When the chiefs arrived in Washington by train in October 1888, they were immediately taken on a whirlwind tour. Sitting Bull had been in Washington during his Wild West days, so that the city's sights were nothing new to him. But those chiefs who had never traveled before were greatly impressed, as government officials had hoped they would be. Most of the chiefs also enthusiastically took up that American craze, cigarette smoking, although Sitting Bull preferred cigars.

Once again Sitting Bull had little to say in public but a lot to say in private. The government had upped their offer to $1 an acre, and some of Sitting Bull's fellow chiefs were beginning to weaken. Sitting Bull had said from the start that the land shouldn't be sold for any amount, but now he argued that the

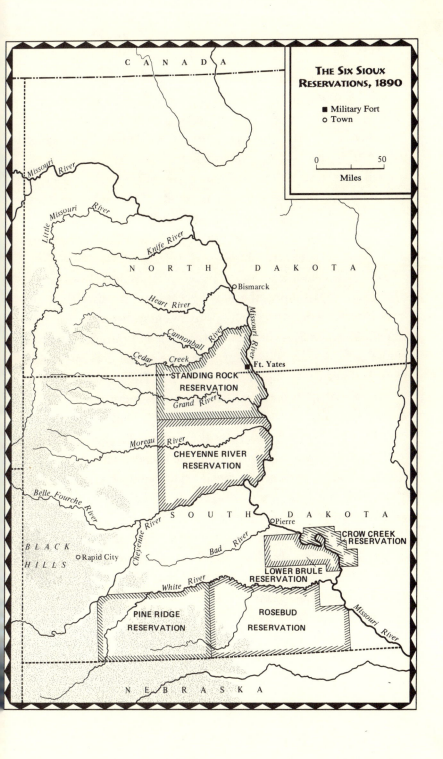

THE SIX SIOUX
RESERVATIONS, 1890

■ Military Fort
○ Town

0   50
Miles

CANADA

Missouri River

Little Missouri River

Knife River

N O R T H   D A K O T A

Heart River

○ Bismarck

Cannonball River

Cedar Creek

Missouri River

■ Ft. Yates

STANDING ROCK
RESERVATION

Grand River

Moreau River

CHEYENNE RIVER
RESERVATION

Belle Fourche River

S O U T H   D A K O T A

○ Pierre

CROW CREEK
RESERVATION

B L A C K
H I L L S   ○ Rapid City

Cheyenne River

Bad River

LOWER BRULE
RESERVATION

White River

PINE RIDGE
RESERVATION

ROSEBUD
RESERVATION

Missouri River

N E B R A S K A

price should be $1.25. It may be that he changed his mind because he didn't believe that the government would agree to such a high figure. And the government didn't. After a quick handshake with the president, Sitting Bull and the other chiefs returned home with nothing settled.

Still determined, the following year Congress passed the Sioux Act of 1889. The new act promised the Sioux $1.25 an acre for land homesteaded by whites during the first three years, seventy-five cents an acre for the next two years, and fifty cents an acre after that.

Yet another commission traveled west in July 1889 to talk the Sioux into signing the new agreement. Because the commissioners visited the other Sioux agencies first, by the time they arrived at Standing Rock they needed only six hundred signatures. To the Sioux' surprise, one of the commissioners was well known to them. It was General Three Stars Crook.

To soften up resistance, the commissioners put on lavish feasts and allowed the Sioux to hold their traditional dances, which had been forbidden by the Indian Bureau. As before, Sitting Bull was in charge behind the scenes, while Gall, John Grass, Mad Bear, and Big Head once again acted as spokesmen. But the four men's objections somehow didn't sound quite as convincing as they had the year before.

Sitting Bull might have mentioned a figure of $1.25 in Washington, but now that he was back at Standing Rock, he staunchly protested selling the land at any price. Although he had assumed that everyone else was still opposed to the offer, he gradually became aware that more and more of his people were seriously discussing whether or not to sign. As supreme chief, he urged, argued, and scolded.

"This land is ours and we must be careful with it. When you lose this land you are going to be beggars," he contended. "If you don't listen to my words you will be herded and driven like animals."

He also relied on his favorite form of persuasion. Used-As-a-Shield described how Sitting Bull strengthened his people's will: "Sitting Bull used to go around the camp circle every evening just before sun set on his favorite horse singing this song:

> " '*The tribe named me*
> *So in courage*
> *I shall live.*' "

At least Sitting Bull knew that he could count on the Silent Eaters. In a long speech, Sitting Bull told them that the *Wasichus* "will try to gain possession of the last piece of ground we possess . . . My Friends and Relatives, let us stand as one family as we had done, before the white people had led us astray."

But Indian agent McLaughlin was also working behind the scenes. McLaughlin even invited Sitting Bull into his office for a whiskey to soften him up. Furious, Sitting Bull grabbed McLaughlin by the neck. "Don't you ever offer me anything like that to make me feel bad," he raged.

McLaughlin's next tactic was to meet secretly with Sitting Bull's four spokesmen, one by one. And one by one, Gall, John Grass, Mad Bear, and Big Head caved in and touched the pen to the government agreement. Following their lead, the other Sioux men lined up to sign, too.

Sitting Bull exploded at the betrayal of the four men whom he had trusted. Mounting his horse and calling on twenty Silent Eaters to accompany him, he galloped into the crowd of would-be signers and scattered them. But McLaughlin had anticipated just such a stunt from the man whom he called Bull and he had alerted the Indian police. Commanded by Lieutenant Bull Head, the mounted Metal Breasts quickly broke up the Silent Eaters' charge.

Bull Head must have felt great satisfaction in routing Sitting Bull and his elite Silent Eaters. Three years before, Sitting Bull had publicly humiliated Bull Head by taking a gift horse away from him and giving it to Bull Head's bitter enemy, Catch-the-Bear. "No matter what Indian he is—if you do him harm, he'll not forget it 'till he gets revenge," observed a fellow Hunkpapa.

Twice more Sitting Bull tried to stampede the men who were waiting to sign, and twice more he failed. Then it was over. By the time Three Stars Crook and the other commissioners returned to Washington in August 1889, more than three-quarters of the Sioux male population had touched the pen to what was called the "Three Stars Treaty."

Half of the Great Sioux Reservation was broken up into six agencies. The other half was to be thrown open to white settlement. A wise old warrior reflected on their loss: "They made us many promises, more than I can remember, but they never kept but one; they promised to take our land and they took it."

Sitting Bull's reaction was more passionate. When he was asked how the Indians felt about losing their land, he snapped, "Indians! There are no Indians left but me!"

◂ 28 ▸

Mother, hand me my sharp knife,
Mother, hand me my sharp knife,
Here come the buffalo returning—
Mother, hand me my sharp knife.

Ghost Dance Song

The Hunkpapas called 1889 "Three-Stars-Came-to-Buy-Lands" in their picture calendar. The event ushered in desperate times. The loss of Sioux land bitterly divided the people between those who had signed the agreement and those, like Sitting Bull, who had not.

The following year brought more despair. Sitting Bull predicted that the crops would be destroyed by terrible heat and hot summer winds, and they were. At the same time, the government drastically cut back on food rations so that starvation haunted all six agencies. Many Sioux sickened and died from the *Wasichu* diseases: measles, whooping cough, and influenza. Unable to hunt, go to war, or ride freely, the Sioux were helpless bystanders to the destruction of their way of life.

The two white women Mary Collins and Catherine Weldon

sympathized with Sitting Bull, his people, and their tragic situation. Catherine Weldon, who had made herself increasingly useful to Sitting Bull, moved into his tipi along with her young son. An artist of no great talent, she even painted his portrait.

But Sitting Bull had always made news, and Catherine's new living arrangements caused quite a stir. The public called her "female crank," "meddlesome busybody," and worse. Because Catherine acted as Sitting Bull's secretary, cooked, cleaned, and did other household chores for him, the Hunkpapas called her Woman-Walking-Ahead. As for Sitting Bull, he assumed that Catherine would become his wife, a suggestion that Catherine flatly rejected.

The two white women may have been sympathetic to the Sioux' plight, but there was little they could do. And then hope arrived from another source.

To the west, in Nevada, a holy man named Wovoka promised that if Indians followed his Ghost Dance religion, the good life would return. Loved ones who had died would come back and speak to them, homelands would be restored, game would once again be plentiful, whites would disappear, there would be no more starvation and sickness, and all tribes would live in peace. Since there was a kernel of Christianity in the Ghost Dance religion, many called Wovoka the Messiah.

Curious about this new religion, Sitting Bull invited the Miniconjou Kicking Bear, a leader in the Ghost Dance, to come to Standing Rock and preach. He arrived in October 1890.

The people were to pray, dance the Ghost Dance, and sing Ghost Dance songs, Kicking Bear instructed. While dancing they were to wear a special garment called a Ghost Shirt. Painted with the sun, moon, stars, birds, and other animals, the shirts would protect them against white bullets. When the dancers "died" (fainted), their dead ancestors, relatives, and friends would appear to them. If the people practiced their faith all winter, the Messiah promised that they would be lifted up in the spring of 1891 to a better life than they had ever known.

Recognizing trouble when he saw it, McLaughlin had Kicking Bear expelled from Standing Rock. He was too late. The some two hundred Hunkpapas in Sitting Bull's Grand River settlement were already in the grip of this new religion. They took their children out of school, moved from log cabins into tipis, and erected a sacred prayer tree and leafy shelter that resembled the old Sun Dance circle. After purifying themselves in a sweat bath, painting their faces, and placing an eagle feather in their hair, the Hunkpapa men and women danced. They joined hands and sang, whirled, stomped, and leapt, all at fever pitch.

Even though Sitting Bull may have longed to once again see his parents and the four children he had lost, he never danced. Nor did he ever serve as Director of the Dance. Nevertheless, he was always open to any religion that might offer medicine or personal power to his people, and he encouraged them to dance. Setting up a tipi close by the Dance circle, he interpreted what the dancers had seen when they "died."

Not only did the Ghost Dance give the Hunkpapas hope, but it also raised Sitting Bull back into a position of power. Over the years, McLaughlin had whittled away at Sitting Bull's influence, turning Gall, Lone Man, and other boyhood companions against him.

"The Indians were encouraged to tell falsehoods about Sitting Bull because the agent didn't like him," Robert Higheagle recalled. Now Sitting Bull's leadership in the Ghost Dance was changing all that.

The Ghost Dance also changed Sitting Bull's relationship with the two white women. Deeply distressed by the Ghost Dance, Catherine Weldon begged Sitting Bull to call a halt to the dancing. When he refused, she left Standing Rock, never to return.

The missionary Mary Collins was even more opposed to the dancing. She once set up her organ near the Dance circle, and although she and her little flock of converts loudly sang "Nearer My God to Thee," they were drowned out by the drums, songs, and wails of the dancers. Confronting Sitting Bull, she scolded him. He was deceiving his people and he knew it. He must stop this nonsense at once.

Sitting Bull didn't interfere with Mary Collins's religion and he saw no reason why she should interfere with his. "Sister," he told her, "I cannot do it. I have come too far."

They all had come too far. The Sioux had always been gamblers. Now they were gambling everything on the Ghost Dance to deliver them from their misery. But their frenzied dancing frightened white settlers, some of whom fled their homes. Others pleaded with the Army to put an end to the Ghost Dance once and for all.

Because the dancing at Standing Rock was pretty much limited to those Hunkpapas living in the Grand River settlement,

McLaughlin wasn't overly concerned. He was concerned, though, that Sitting Bull's leadership role in the Ghost Dance was an increasing threat to his authority. Ever since Sitting Bull had arrived, the two men had competed as to which one was head chief at Standing Rock.

To be rid of his rival, McLaughlin wrote to the Indian office in Washington, requesting that Sitting Bull be arrested. Vain, cunning, pompous, cowardly, liar, and chief mischief-maker were only some of the charges McLaughlin hurled at Sitting Bull in his letter. But Sitting Bull was still a national celebrity with friends and sympathizers back east, and government officials feared their reaction if Sitting Bull was arrested. The answer came back. No.

Taking matters into his own hands, on November 17, McLaughlin headed for Grand River, accompanied by an interpreter and Sitting Bull's archenemy, the Metal Breast Lieutenant Bull Head. This Ghost Dance religion is rubbish, McLaughlin thundered at Sitting Bull in a long tirade. It will bring nothing but grief, and the dancers will all be punished for it.

Sitting Bull, who had just emerged from a sweat bath, kept his composure. "You go with me to the agencies to the West," he suggested. "Let me seek for the men who saw the Messiah; and when we find them, I will demand that they show him to us, and if they cannot do so I will return and tell my people it is a lie."

That would be like trying to catch the wind that blew last year, McLaughlin protested. After about an hour, when he realized that he wasn't making any progress, McLaughlin climbed back into his wagon. But the dancers swarmed around him, jeering and muttering threats. With a raised arm, Sitting Bull quieted the menacing mob in a show of power that let McLaughlin know just who was headman, at least at the Grand River settlement.

Now all McLaughlin could do was wait for the Plains winter weather to call a halt to the dancing. But once again Sitting Bull had the last word. Always a remarkably accurate forecaster, Sitting Bull reassured the Hunkpapas, "Yes, my people, you can dance all winter this year. The sun will shine warmly and the weather will be fair."

It was one of the warmest winters that anyone could remember.

Meanwhile, the dancing had gotten out of control at the Pine Ridge and Rosebud agencies. With the Metal Breasts unable to handle the situation, the Indian agents called for the Army to step in. From his Chicago office, that all-too-familiar figure Bear Coat Miles, now a general, ordered troops to march into both Pine Ridge and Rosebud.

But the soldiers couldn't stop the dancers. Escaping to a protected high plateau on the Pine Ridge Agency that became known as the Stronghold, the people continued to dance. While the military tried to figure out how to get them down without an armed confrontation, reporters kept the nation on edge with sensational stories of an impending war.

Although the Grand River dancers got word of the Army invasion, they didn't stop dancing either. McLaughlin, however, was beginning to realize that the Ghost Dance was more of a threat than he first had thought. Hoping that one of his own people would be able to talk Sitting Bull into controlling the dancers, McLaughlin sent the Metal Breast Lone Man to Grand River. Lone Man started their meeting by recalling old times when he had followed Sitting Bull into battle.

"Yes, I depended on you then, but now you have turned with the whites against me. I have nothing more to say to you," Sitting Bull retorted. "So far as I am concerned, you may go home."

On November 24, Bear Coat Miles, who was determined to see his old adversary in irons, ordered Buffalo Bill Cody to travel to Standing Rock and arrest Sitting Bull. Both McLaughlin and Colonel William Drum, the commanding officer of Fort Yates, predicted even more trouble if Buffalo Bill tried to arrest his former Wild West pal. Together they managed to keep Buffalo Bill away from Sitting Bull until McLaughlin could contact officials in Washington and have Miles's bizarre plan cancelled.

Furious at being thwarted, on December 10, Miles commanded Colonel Drum to make the arrest himself. Still Drum hesitated. Both he and McLaughlin were afraid that at the first sign of soldiers, the dancers would either join their Sioux cousins in the Stronghold or they would establish their own Stronghold.

Meanwhile, Sitting Bull wanted to learn more about the Ghost Dance, and the Miniconjou Kicking Bear was the one who could teach him. Besides, he had heard rumors that McLaughlin planned to have him arrested and it might be best if he was gone from Standing Rock for a while. Backed by his Silent Eaters, Sitting Bull made arrangements to leave.

163

On December 12, McLaughlin received a letter that Sitting Bull had dictated to his son-in-law. In it, Sitting Bull not only urged McLaughlin to allow his people to practice their own religion as the whites did, but he also requested a pass to leave Standing Rock and visit the Pine Ridge Agency.

When McLaughlin received Sitting Bull's request to visit Pine Ridge, he and Drum made their own arrangements. On December 14 they put out an order for the Metal Breasts to arrest Sitting Bull. The date and time were set: the next morning before dawn.

· 29 ·

Sitting Bull, you have always been a brave man;
What is going to happen to us now?

Four Robes's Song of Lament

In the dark hours before dawn on December 15, 1890, Sitting Bull was asleep. With him in his one-room cabin were his wife Four Robes, their young child, the fourteen-year-old Crow Foot, One Bull's wife, and two old men guests. Outside, on a raw and drizzly morning, the clattering approach of horses over the frozen ground set the Grand River settlement's packs of dogs to barking. A loud knock on Sitting Bull's cabin door woke everyone up. It was a little before six.

"Sitting Bull!" came a shout.

Recently Sitting Bull had posted bodyguards around his cabin, but the previous night, he and his guards had talked of old times until late, and he had sent them home. The door banged open and dark forms pushed into the room. A match flared and a candle was lit.

Grabbing her child, Four Robes cried out, "What are you jealous people doing here?"

The *ceska maza* Lieutenant Bull Head ignored her. He turned to Sitting Bull. "I come after you to take you to the Agency. You are under arrest."

"How, all right," Sitting Bull answered calmly.

If Sitting Bull was calm, his family wasn't. As more Metal Breasts spilled into the room, One Bull's wife and the two old men fled. Crow Foot stood his ground stubbornly, but Four Robes, still holding her child, began to wail her anguish.

The Metal Breasts, who wore strips of white cloth around their necks so that they would recognize each other in the dark, were excited, too. They had been willing to follow McLaughlin's orders, but, face-to-face with their old chief, they found that making the arrest wasn't so easy.

Some had been Sitting Bull's childhood friends. Others had followed him into battle, while still others had spent four years with him in Canada. And Four Robes's loud keening only added to their nervousness. Even though Sitting Bull was still naked from sleep, the Metal Breasts hustled him toward the door.

"This is a great way to do things," he protested. "Not to give me a chance to put on my clothes in winter time."

The Metal Breasts told Four Robes to run and fetch her husband's clothes from the other cabin, where the rest of his family were sleeping. When Four Robes returned, the Metal Breasts hurried Sitting Bull into blue leggings, a white shirt, and moccasins. As soon as he was dressed, the Metal Breasts once again prodded him toward the door.

166

Sitting Bull jerked away from their grip. "Let me go," he ordered. "I'll go without any assistance."

McLaughlin had directed Bull Head to transport Sitting Bull in a wagon the forty miles back to the agency. But on his own, Bull Head had commanded a Metal Breast to saddle up Sitting Bull's prized Wild West horse and bring him around to the cabin door. With his breath snorting clouds of white in the cold gray of the breaking dawn, the horse was held in readiness.

Also waiting in the misty drizzle were some 150 of Sitting Bull's most loyal supporters, the Grand River Ghost Dancers. Awakened from sleep by the barking dogs, the *rat-a-tat* of horses' hooves, and Four Robes's loud lamentations, the people had run from their homes to gather outside Sitting Bull's cabin. Cursing and shouting taunts, the angry crowd pressed against the line of Metal Breasts that held them back. And when Sitting Bull came through the door with Lieutenant Bull Head on one side, Sergeant Shave Head on the other, and Sergeant Red Tomahawk behind him, a howl of rage went up.

The situation was escalating out of control. It was just what McLaughlin and Colonel Drum had wanted to avoid. They had intended for Bull Head and his *ceska maza* to arrest Sitting Bull quietly and head back to the agency before the rest of Grand River was even awake. Now it was too late. In a shouting–shoving uproar, Sitting Bull's people hurled threats at the little band of forty-three Metal Breasts.

"Kill them! Kill them!" Crawler shouted.

Someone else cried, "*Hopo, Hopo,* kill the old police first and the young will flee."

"Let him go!" Strikes-the-Kettle yelled. "Leave him alone!"

Chief of Sitting Bull's bodyguards, Catch-the-Bear, shouldered his way through the excited mob to confront his old enemy Bull Head. "Now here are the *ceska maza* just as we had expected all the time," he scoffed. "You think you are going to take him. You shall not do it. Come on now, let us protect our Chief." And he waved the crowd on.

As the Ghost Dancers surged forward with a roar, Crow Foot suddenly appeared in the cabin doorway. "Well, you always called yourself a brave chief," he called to his father. "Now you are allowing yourself to be taken by the *ceska maza*."

Crow Foot was Sitting Bull's favorite son. He had accompanied his father to many councils. And it was Crow Foot who had surrendered Sitting Bull's Winchester to the commanding officer at Fort Buford nine years ago. Now his son's scorn caught Sitting Bull up short. And he was moved by his frightened wife's mournful song.

> *"Sitting Bull, you have always been a brave man;*
> *What is going to happen to us now?"*

Perhaps Sitting Bull also remembered another song, a song that his friend the meadowlark had sung to him: *"The Sioux will kill you."* No, he would stand firm and remain here among his comrades and loved ones.

"I am not going," he said defiantly. "Do with me what you please. I am not going."

"Come now, do not listen to anyone," Bull Head ordered.

"Uncle, no one is going to harm you. The Agent wants to see you and then you are to come back," the Metal Breast Lone

Man lied, "so please do not let others lead you into any trouble."

Behind him, Sergeant Red Tomahawk barked a warning: "You have no ears."

Fearful for Sitting Bull's life, Jumping Bull, who had raced to the scene, tried to persuade the man who had once saved his life to go quietly.

"No, I'm not going," Sitting Bull repeated.

Once Sitting Bull's mind was made up, there was no changing it. All the Metal Breasts knew that. Bull Head pulled at Sitting Bull's left arm, while Red Tomahawk shoved him from behind.

At that, Sitting Bull shouted out, "Come on everybody!"

"By this time the whole camp was in commotion," the Metal Breast Lone Man reported later. "Women and children crying while the men gathered all around us. The police tried to keep order was useless—it was like trying to extinguish a treacherous prairie fire."

"You shall not take our chief," came a cry.

With that, Catch-the-Bear pulled a Winchester from under his blanket, aimed, and fired at Bull Head. The bullet struck him in the left side. Twisting as he fell, Bull Head drew a revolver and shot Sitting Bull in the chest at point-blank range. As Sitting Bull slumped, Red Tomahawk fired, too. The bullet struck Sitting Bull in the back of the head.

He died instantly. Either shot would have killed him. At the sight of their fallen chief, the frenzied mob stampeded, attacking the Metal Breasts with guns, knives, and clubs. Catch-the-Bear aimed his Winchester at Lone Man, but his rifle misfired.

Lone Man grabbed the rifle, smashed Catch-the-Bear over the head, and then shot him. The bright flare of rifle sparks lit up the dark haze of gunsmoke.

Within minutes the slaughter was over. The Ghost Dancers raced for the nearby woods, while the Metal Breasts ran to take up a defensive position in Sitting Bull's sheds and corral. Other Metal Breasts carried the wounded Bull Head, Middle, and Shave Head into Sitting Bull's cabin. As they laid Bull Head on the bed, the Metal Breast Running Hawk pointed to the far wall.

"Say, my friends," he said, "it seems there is something moving behind the curtain in the corner of the cabin."

It was Crow Foot.

"My uncles, do not kill me," the boy begged. "I do not wish to die."

Bull Head, who had been struck by four bullets, knew that he was fatally wounded. Now, when he was asked what Crow Foot's fate should be, he pronounced a death sentence: "Kill him; they killed me."

Lone Man cracked Crow Foot on the head with his rifle butt. The boy staggered and fell. Together Lone Man, One Feather, and Red Tomahawk dragged Crow Foot from the cabin and filled his body with bullets as they wept.

Sitting Bull's saddled Wild West horse still stood by the door among the carnage. It was later rumored that the horse had sat on his haunches at the first sound of gunshots and raised his hoof, just as if Sitting Bull's spirit had entered his body.

Ordered by Red Tomahawk to alert the Army troops that were stationed in readiness not far away, Hawk Man mounted Sitting Bull's horse and rode off. Although the Ghost Dancers fired at him from a grove of trees, they failed to stop him. From Sitting Bull's outbuildings, the Metal Breasts shot back at the Ghost Dancers. The two sides exchanged gunfire until the troops arrived and aimed their howitzer into the woods. At the heavy artillery barrage, the Ghost Dancers fled, running through the willows and up into the hills.

The Long Knives found a scene of bloody horror. Sitting Bull, Crow Foot, Jumping Bull, Jumping Bull's son, Catch-the-Bear, Blackbird, Spotted-Horn-Bull, Brave Thunder, and two horses had been killed. Inside the cabin, four Metal Breasts lay dead. Although Middle recovered, Bull Head and Shave Head were both to die soon. Even Catherine Weldon's portrait of Sitting Bull had been slashed by a Metal Breast mourning his fallen brother.

Sitting Bull's supporters had escaped at the first sign of the Long Knives, all but the courageous Crow Woman. Dressed in his red Ghost Shirt and riding a fine black horse, he galloped out of the woods to demonstrate that his Ghost Shirt was indeed bulletproof.

> *"Father, I thought you said*
> *We were all going to live,"*

he sang as bullets flew around him. Twice more Crow Woman charged out singing, and twice more he rode off unharmed through a hail of gunfire. And then he disappeared into the woods. "The Battle in the Dark" was over.

Two days later, on December 17, 1890, the slain Metal Breasts were buried in the Standing Rock cemetery with full military honors, a three-volley gun salute, and the playing of taps.

Shortly afterward, another burial took place, this one in the Fort Yates military cemetery. The grave had been dug by four Army prisoners from the guardhouse. With only McLaughlin and three Army officers present, Sitting Bull's body, wrapped in canvas and placed in a crude wooden box, was hauled from the Dead House to the grave in a two-wheeled cart pulled by a mule. Silently the box was lowered into the grave, with no honors at all.

As son, husband, father, friend, holy man, hunter, composer, singer, and war chief of the Sioux Nation, Sitting Bull had garnered honors throughout his lifetime. A simple wooden board with the words "Sitting Bull, Indian" burned into it marked his grave. Perhaps the man who had died only a few miles from where he had been born fifty-nine years before would have prized that title above all.

> *"Friends, take fresh courage*
> *This is my country I loved."*
> *Sitting Bull, saying this, has passed away.*
>
> *"Friends, take courage*
> *As for me, I'm helpless."*
> *Sitting Bull, saying this, has passed away.*

Hunkpapa Song Dedicated
to Sitting Bull

Bibliography

Adams, Alexander B. *Sitting Bull: A Biography*. New York: G. P. Putnam's Sons, 1973.

Anderson, Harry H. "Indian Peace-Talkers and the Conclusion of the Sioux War of 1876." *Nebraska History*. Lincoln, NE: Nebraska State Historical Society, December 1963, Vol. 44, No. 4, pp. 233–254.

Armstrong, Virginia Irving. *I Have Spoken: American History Through the Voices of Indians*. Chicago: The Swallow Press, Inc., 1971.

Bourke, John G. *On the Border with Crook*. Lincoln, NE: University of Nebraska Press, 1971.

Brown, Joseph Epes. *The Sacred Pipe: Black Elk's Account of the Seven Rites of the Oglala Sioux*. Norman, OK, and London: University of Oklahoma Press, 1953.

Campbell, Walter S. *Walter S. Campbell Collection*. Boxes 104, 105, 106, 112, 113, 114. Norman, OK: University of Oklahoma.

Carroll, John M., ed. *The Arrest and Killing of Sitting Bull: A Documentary*. Privately printed, The Arthur H. Clark Company, 1986.

De Barthe, Joe, ed., Edgar I. Stewart. *Life and Adventures of Frank Grouard*. Norman, OK: University of Oklahoma Press, 1958.

Densmore, Frances. *Teton Sioux Music and Culture*. Lincoln, NE: University of Nebraska Press, 1992.

De Smet, Father Pierre-Jean. *Life, Letters and Travels of Father Pierre-Jean De Smet, S.J. 1801–1873*. Edited by Hiram M. Chittenden and Alfred T. Richardson. Vols. 1, 3, 4. New York: Kraus Reprint Co., 1969.

Finerty, John F. *War-Path and Bivouac*. Norman, OK: University of Oklahoma Press, 1961.

Frost, Lawrence A. *The Custer Album*. Seattle: Superior Publishing Company, 1964.

Graham, Colonel W. A. *The Custer Myth: A Source Book of Custeriana*. New York: Bonanza Books, 1953.

Greene, Jerome A., ed. *Battles and Skirmishes of the Great Sioux War, 1876–1877*. Norman, OK: University of Oklahoma Press, 1993.

Grinnell, George Bird. *The Fighting Cheyennes*. New York: Charles Scribner's Sons, 1915.

———. *When Buffalo Ran*. New Haven: Yale University Press, 1920.

Hardorff, Richard, ed. *Lakota Recollections of the Custer Fight: New Sources of Indian-Military History*. Spokane: The Arthur H. Clark Company, 1991.

Hassrick, Royal B. *The Sioux, Life and Customs of a Warrior Society*. Norman, OK: University of Oklahoma Press, 1964.

Hook, Jason. *Sitting Bull and the Plains Indians*. New York: The Bookwright Press, 1987.

Hoover, Herbert T., and Robert C. Hollow. *The Last Years of Sitting Bull*. Bismarck: State Historical Society of North Dakota, 1984.

Hyde, George. *Red Cloud's Folk, A History of the Oglala Sioux Indians*. Norman, OK: University of Oklahoma Press, 1937.

Johnson, W. Fletcher. *Life of Sitting Bull and History of the Indian War of 1890–91*. Edgewood Publishing Company, 1891.

MacEwan, Grant. *Sitting Bull—The Years in Canada*. Edmonton, AB: Hurtig Publishers, 1973.

McGinnis, Anthony. *Counting Coup and Cutting Horses: Intertribal Warfare on the Northern Plains, 1738–1889*. Evergreen, CO: Cordillera Press, Inc., 1990.

McLaughlin, James. *My Friend the Indian*. Lincoln, NE: University of Nebraska Press, 1989.

Manzione, Joseph. *"I Am Looking to the North For My Life": Sitting Bull 1876–1881*. Salt Lake City: University of Utah Press, 1991.

Maxwell, James A., ed. *America's Fascinating Indian Heritage*. Pleasantville, NY: The Reader's Digest Association, Inc., 1978.

Nabokov, Peter, ed. *Native American Testimony*. New York: Viking Penguin, 1978.

Neihardt, John G. *Black Elk Speaks*. Lincoln, NE: University of Nebraska Press, 1979.

Remele, Larry, ed. *Fort Buford and the Military Frontier on the Northern Plains*. Bismarck, ND: State Historical Society of North Dakota, 1987.

Robinson, Doane. *A History of the Dakota or Sioux Indians*. Minneapolis: Ross & Haines, Inc., 1904.

Rosa, Joseph G., and Robin May. *Buffalo Bill and His Wild West*. Lawrence, KS: University Press of Kansas, 1989.

Russell, Don. *The Lives and Legends of Buffalo Bill*. Norman, OK: University of Oklahoma Press, 1960.

St. George, Judith. *Crazy Horse*. New York: G. P. Putnam's Sons, 1994.

Standing Bear, Luther. *Land of the Spotted Eagle*. Lincoln, NE: University of Nebraska Press, 1978.

———. *My Indian Boyhood*. Lincoln, NE: University of Nebraska Press, 1988.

———. *My People the Sioux*. Boston: Houghton Mifflin Co., Inc., 1928.

Stewart, Edgar I. *Custer's Luck*. Norman, OK: University of Oklahoma Press, 1955.

Utley, Robert M. *Custer Battlefield, A History and Guide to the Battle of the Little Bighorn*. Washington, D.C.: National Park Service, Division of Publications, 1988.

———. *Frontier Regulars*. New York: Macmillan Publishing Co., Inc., 1973.

———. *Frontiersmen in Blue 1848–1865*. New York: The Macmillan Company, 1967.

———. *The Lance and the Shield: The Life and Times of Sitting Bull*. New York: Henry Holt and Company, 1993.

———. *The Last Days of the Sioux Nation*. New Haven: Yale University Press, 1963.

Vestal, Stanley. *New Sources of Indian History, 1850–1891.* Norman, OK: University of Oklahoma Press, 1934.

———. *Sitting Bull, Champion of the Sioux.* Norman, OK: University of Oklahoma Press, 1957.

———. *Warpath and Council Fire.* New York: Random House, 1948.

Index